The Final Reflection

Shadows of Justice

Victoria S. Grant

Table of Contents

Chapter 1
Eerie Beginnings

In the dim light of early morning, Detective Ian Mercer's car rolled to a stop at the edge of Willow's Bridge. The scene was quiet, the only sounds were the distant calls of morning birds and the soft hum of the river below. As Ian stepped out, the chill of the river mist brushed against his face, a stark contrast to the warmth inside his vehicle. He buttoned up his coat and approached the fluttering police tape that cordoned off the area.

The bridge, an old structure of weathered stone and iron, had seen many a whispered secret between its arches. Today, it held a silence that was both solemn and expectant as if the river itself paused to mourn. The police officers on site nodded at Ian with a respect born of many shared cases, their faces somber, eyes avoiding the body that lay covered at the center of the bridge.

"Morning, Detective," greeted Officer Jim Reynolds, his breath misting in the cold air. "Didn't expect to see you here this early."

Ian nodded, his gaze fixed on the covered form. "What do we have?"

"Victim's a local school teacher, mid-thirties, found by a jogger around dawn. No witnesses so far. Looks like a jump, but with these things, you never know," Jim explained, handing Ian a pair of gloves.

As Ian approached the body, the other officers stepped back, giving him space. He crouched down, his fingers trembling slightly—not from the cold, but from the anticipation of what was to come. Carefully, he lifted the corner of the white sheet. The victim's face was peaceful, almost as if she were asleep, except for the eyes. Those eyes that stared emptily into the void would have haunted any other man, but for Ian, they were a gateway.

He reached out, touching her cold hand gently with his own, grounding himself for the vision that would come. His gift—or curse, as he sometimes thought of it—allowed him a glimpse into the final moments of the person's life whose eyes he met post-mortem.

The flood of images was instantaneous. The school teacher, her face distorted by fear, her hands grappling with an unseen assailant. The struggle was violent, her eyes wide with terror, not resignation. The scene shifted rapidly, a disjointed series of noises and colors that ended abruptly with the cold, dark water below.

Ian stood, his heart pounding, his breath short. It was not suicide. It was murder, staged to look like a desperate escape from life.

He turned to Jim, his voice steady despite the chaos in his mind. "This wasn't a suicide. She was frightened, fighting for her life. We're looking at a homicide."

Jim's eyebrows shot up, but he didn't question Ian's judgment. "I'll call the captain. We'll need the full team."

As the first rays of dawn lightened the sky, casting long shadows across the bridge, Ian's silhouette stood tall and resolute. The investigation would start here, on this quiet bridge with its whispered secrets. And Ian Mercer would unravel the truth, no matter how deep he had to dive into the dark waters of Willow's End.

The Willow's End Police Department arrived in full force, bringing with them the solemnity and precision that such scenes demanded. Crime scene tape expanded, encircling a wider perimeter around Willow's Bridge, while uniformed officers directed the sparse early morning traffic away from the area. The somber task of cataloging the scene had begun, the flash of cameras punctuating the morning air as forensic experts moved meticulously.

Detective Ian Mercer surveyed the area with a critical eye, his mind racing with the implications of his vision. Each detail could be a clue, a silent witness to the tragedy that had unfolded under the cover of darkness. The victim's belongings were laid out on a white sheet near where her body had been found—a purse, keys, a small, neatly folded scarf, and a book, the title obscured by the angle.

"Detective, take a look at this," called out Detective Sarah Langley, Ian's partner, who had been examining the surroundings near the railing. She pointed to a set of scuff marks on the old stone barrier, barely discernible against the weathered surface. "These could be from her shoes. Looks like she struggled or was held back against the railing."

Ian joined her, kneeling to get a closer look. "Good catch," he murmured, his fingers tracing the marks lightly. The pattern was inconsistent with someone climbing over voluntarily. The abrasions suggested a chaotic, desperate movement, aligning with the terror he had seen in the teacher's eyes.

"Anything on the ground?" Ian asked, standing to scan the area where the earth met the base of the bridge.

"A few fibers, maybe from her coat or from the assailant. We've bagged them for analysis," Sarah replied, her voice low, matching the gravity of their findings. She handed him a plastic evidence bag containing a few strands of bright fabric—strikingly red against the dark soil.

"This doesn't match her clothing," Ian noted, holding the bag up to the light. "She was wearing dark colors."

"Exactly. I've already sent a sample to the lab. Should tell us if someone else was here with her," Sarah said, her eyes scanning the horizon thoughtfully.

The rising sun cast a golden glow over the scene, the light stretching long and thin across the bridge deck. Ian's gaze followed the trajectory of the shadows, noting how each crevice and crack on the worn stone seemed to hold a secret. He walked slowly across the bridge, each step deliberate, pausing occasionally to crouch and inspect something on the ground—a discarded cigarette butt, a small, crumpled receipt blown against the base of a lamp post.

"Anything else out of place?" Ian called out to the team.

"Not much else that stands out," one of the forensic techs called back. "We'll need to wait for the autopsy for more."

Nodding, Ian walked back to the body's initial location, his mind replaying the vision. The struggle, the fear—it was all here, but the serene setup betrayed the violence of her last moments. Why stage it as a suicide? What message were they trying to send, or what truth were they trying to bury?

As he pondered, Sarah approached, her tablet in hand. "Here's something you need to see, Ian. The victim's phone was locked, but we managed to bypass it. Look at her last messages," she said, handing him the device.

Ian scrolled through the texts, his brow furrowing. The conversation was with an unknown number, the exchange tense, cryptic. Phrases like "Can't do this anymore" and "Meet me at the bridge at dawn" popped out, stark against the glowing screen.

"Looks like she was lured here," Ian muttered, handing back the tablet. "Or she was trying to meet someone to end something dangerous."

"Or both," Sarah added, her voice tinged with a mix of frustration and intrigue. "I'm going to dig deeper into her call logs, see if we can trace this number."

Ian nodded, his eyes once again sweeping over the bridge. The sun had fully risen now, its light erasing the shadows and bathing the bridge in an almost picturesque quality. But the darkness of the crime lay heavy on the waters below, and on his shoulders.

As the team continued their work, Ian stood by the railing, looking down at the rushing water. The river knew the truth, and soon, he would too. The day was just beginning, and there was much to uncover. The scene before him was like a meticulously crafted stage—every prop and player perfectly placed, yet the story they told was anything but serene.

The early morning light now fully unveiled the grim reality of the bridge, transforming it from a place of spectral half-shadows into a stark scene of forensic activity. Detective Ian Mercer, his senses sharpened by the chill of the morning air and the weight of his grim discovery, remained by the railing, his gaze occasionally drifting to the river below, which seemed to flow indifferently towards its own unseen destinations.

"Detective Mercer, are you alright?" Sarah Langley's voice cut through his thoughts, her presence a steady force at his side.

Ian turned, offering a brief nod. "Just thinking about the next steps. We need to understand the motive behind this staging. Her terror was palpable, Sarah. It wasn't just fear of death; it was dread of something worse."

Sarah looked towards the water, then back at Ian. "Her phone records might give us more to go on. But about what you saw... Can you describe it again?"

Ian hesitated, the memory vivid and visceral. "It's like watching a nightmare unfold. She was on this bridge, fighting against someone. I couldn't see who—it was more like a shadow or a blur. But the terror in her eyes was clear. And then, a push... It wasn't just physical; it was a betrayal."

"Betrayal?" Sarah echoed, her brow furrowing as she considered his words. "That suggests she knew the person well. Could it be someone from her personal life? A friend, or maybe a lover?"

"Possibly," Ian replied, his voice tinged with uncertainty. "Or it could be someone she trusted in a different capacity. We should look into her connections, both personal and professional. Anyone who might benefit from her death looking like a suicide."

Sarah pulled out her tablet, tapping through screens of information. "I'll start with the staff at her school and her closest known associates. If we can draw a line from her to our suspect, or at least build a profile of her inner circle, it might shed some light on this."

"Good idea," Ian agreed, watching as a forensic officer approached them with a small evidence bag in hand. "What do you have there?"

The officer, a young woman with sharp eyes, held up the bag. "Found this under the bridge, caught on one of the lower beams. It's a piece of torn fabric, looks like from a man's shirt. There's a trace of blood on it."

Ian took the bag, examining the fabric. "This could be from the struggle. Have it analyzed immediately. If we can match the blood to the victim, it might help us identify the assailant if they were injured during the altercation."

"Will do, Detective," the officer responded, making a note on her pad before heading back to her work.

Turning back to Sarah, Ian's expression was grim yet determined. "If they were close enough for her to tear their shirt, this wasn't a random act. This was personal, and it was planned."

Sarah nodded, her mind racing with the implications. "I'll push for a rush on the analysis. In the meantime, let's keep digging into her life. There's more here, I can feel it."

The two detectives returned to the center of the bridge, where the majority of the evidence had been collected. They stood together, surveying the scene, each lost in thought.

"Do you ever wish you couldn't see these things?" Sarah asked quietly, breaking the silence.

"Every time," Ian admitted, his voice barely above a whisper. "But then I remember that without this curse, we might never get to the truth. It's a double-edged sword."

"Let's use it to cut through the lies," Sarah suggested, her tone resolute.

Ian managed a small smile, appreciating her steadfastness. "Exactly."

As the scene was cleared and the morning wore on, the river continued its endless journey past the bridge, uncaring and oblivious to the human dramas that unfolded by its banks. But for Ian Mercer, each clue gathered, each piece of evidence logged, was a step closer to giving voice to the silent plea for justice emanating from the cold depths below. The river might forget, but he would not.

The morning air began to warm as the sun climbed higher, casting light over Willow's Bridge and illuminating the small groups of investigators who moved with purpose and precision. The chaotic urgency of the initial discovery had given way to the meticulous rhythm of routine police work. Crime scene officers measured distances and marked evidence with numbered placards, photographers documented every angle, and the forensic team whispered amongst themselves, piecing together the silent story told by the traces left behind.

Detective Ian Mercer stood slightly apart, his eyes never straying far from the bridge's railing where the victim's life had tragically ended. The fabric sample with traces of blood had been a significant find, one that could potentially lead to the assailant. Ian's mind raced with possibilities, each more disturbing than the last. His unique insight into the victim's final moments painted a vivid picture of her fear and desperation, images that now burned in his memory, urging him forward.

His partner, Detective Sarah Langley, approached from the forensic tent, her face set in a mask of determination. "The lab will expedite the analysis of the fabric and blood. We should have something by tomorrow. Also, the victim's phone records came in; there are a few numbers that need looking into, frequent contacts in the days leading up to her death."

Ian nodded, processing this new information. "Good, follow up on those. I'll take another look at her personal and work environments. There might be something we missed, some connection that explains why she was targeted."

Sarah agreed with a nod, her tablet clutched in one hand as she quickly typed notes with the other. "I'll also revisit the interviews with her colleagues and friends. Someone might have seen or heard something they didn't think was important at the time."

As Sarah walked away to make her calls, Ian turned his attention back to the bridge. The scene had been thoroughly documented and was now being cleared, the normalcy of traffic soon to be restored. But for Ian, the normalcy was a thin veneer over the undercurrent of his thoughts, which continued to swirl dark and deep.

He walked slowly across the bridge, each step deliberate, pausing where the victim's belongings had been found. He crouched, placing his hand on the cold, rough surface of the path, closing his eyes briefly. The bridge was old, a silent witness to countless passings, joyous and sorrowful alike. Now, it bore the weight of another dark tale.

Opening his eyes, Ian stood and made his way back to his car. He pulled out the case file from the passenger seat, flipping it open to review the victim's information again. Her name, her life, her smiling photo paper-clipped to the corner; a life reduced to case notes and witness statements. He traced her name with his finger, a promise forming in his mind—a promise to uncover the truth, no matter where it led or how dangerous the path might be.

Back at the station, Ian's decision to delve deeper into the investigation solidified as he organized his notes and planned his next moves. The victim's relationships, her last known activities, and now, the list of phone contacts—all these formed the pieces of a puzzle that, when completed, would reveal the face of a killer.

He sat at his desk, the bustle of the precinct a distant hum as he focused on the task at hand. Calls to make, leads to follow, a mystery to solve—all driven by the supernatural insight that both blessed and cursed him. This case was personal, not just because of the vision, but because someone had tried to use death to tell a lie. And in Willow's End, lies were like the river—ever flowing, but never clear.

As the day shifted towards afternoon, Ian's resolve grew. The investigation was no longer just a matter of procedure; it was a quest for justice. The bridge would no longer be just a crossing over the river; it would be the place where the truth was revealed, one clue at a time. The work ahead was daunting, the path uncertain, but Detective Ian Mercer was ready to follow wherever it led.

Chapter 2
Seeds of Doubt

The atmosphere inside the Willow's End Police Department was a stark contrast to the quiet, reflective scene at the bridge. Here, the air buzzed with the low hum of conversation, ringing phones, and the occasional clatter of a keyboard. Detective Ian Mercer entered through the double doors, the file containing the case details tucked under his arm, his mind still replaying the morning's discoveries.

As he made his way to the briefing room, his colleagues nodded in his direction, their expressions a mixture of curiosity and concern. The news of the morning's grim findings had already permeated the station, and the usual banter that filled the halls had subdued into hushed tones.

Detective Sarah Langley was already there, setting up her laptop and arranging her notes in preparation for the briefing. She looked up as Ian entered, giving him a brief nod.

"We've got everyone coming in. I think it's crucial we all understand the direction this is taking," she said, her voice firm.

Ian placed his file on the table and leaned against the back of the chair. "Good. They need to see the full picture, not just the fragments. There's more to this than a simple suicide, and I want all hands on deck for this."

As the room filled with officers and detectives, Chief Raymond Harte entered, his presence commanding immediate attention. He took a seat at the head of the table, his eyes scanning the room before settling on Ian.

"Mercer, start us off. What are we looking at here?" Chief Harte's voice was authoritative yet carried an undercurrent of supportive concern.

Ian stood, clearing his throat slightly. "Thank you, Chief. As you all know, this morning we were called to Willow's Bridge on a reported suicide. However, the evidence we've gathered from the scene strongly suggests otherwise. This was not a suicide; it was a staged homicide."

Murmurs filled the room, some of disbelief, others of intrigue. Ian continued, "We found significant signs of struggle, inconsistencies at the scene, and most importantly, a supernatural insight that revealed the victim's terror and struggle before her death."

Sarah chimed in, supporting Ian's statement with the technical evidence. "We've also collected forensic evidence that supports this. There's a piece of torn fabric with blood, found under the bridge, which doesn't belong to the victim. We're running it through the lab now."

Chief Harte held up a hand, silencing the room. "Alright, I understand the gravity of this situation. Mercer, Langley, you two will lead this investigation. I want updates twice a day. This isn't just about solving a crime; it's about preserving the trust of our community. We handle this discreetly and efficiently."

Ian nodded, feeling the weight of the Chief's words. "Understood, Chief. We'll keep the investigation tight and focused. We're also digging into the victim's background, her connections, anything that might give us a lead on why someone would want to stage her death as a suicide."

An older detective raised his hand, a skeptical look on his face. "Ian, you mentioned supernatural insight. Are we really going to base our investigation on... on visions now?"

Ian met the detective's gaze squarely. "It's not the sole basis, but it's a tool—like any other investigative aid we use. My... insights have led us to solid evidence before. I don't ask anyone to believe blindly, but I do ask for your trust in my methods."

The room settled into an uneasy silence as the implications of Ian's abilities mingled with the tangible evidence presented. After a moment, Chief Harte cleared his throat.

"Let's proceed based on the evidence. Keep me posted on the lab results for that fabric and any breaks in the phone records or interviews. Dismissed."

As the meeting adjourned, the officers and detectives filed out, leaving Ian and Sarah to gather their materials. The seeds of doubt had been planted, not just about the nature of the crime, but also about the reliance on unconventional methods in a town that prided itself on its pragmatism.

Stepping out into the corridor, Ian felt the lingering glances of his colleagues, their skepticism a palpable barrier. But his resolve was firm, and as he and Sarah walked back to their desks, their steps were synchronized—a united front in a sea of doubt, ready to delve deeper into the shadows of Willow's End.

Back at their desks, surrounded by the ambient noise of the bustling precinct, Detective Ian Mercer and Detective Sarah Langley hunched over their respective computers. The glow of the screens illuminated their focused expressions as they combed through digital records and personal details of the victim, Eleanor White.

"Here's something interesting," Sarah announced, breaking the silence that had settled between them. She rotated her monitor slightly so Ian could see. "Eleanor was quite active on social media, lots of posts about her work at the school, her volunteer work, but these posts... they change tone dramatically about three weeks ago."

Ian leaned in, studying the shift in language and content. "From cheerful and engaging to... what would you call this? Detached?"

"Exactly," Sarah replied. "It's subtle, but it's there. Could be nothing, or it could be when things started going wrong for her."

"Let's dig deeper into that timeline. See who she was interacting with most during that shift," Ian suggested, turning back to his own screen to pull up Eleanor's phone records.

As he scrolled through the call logs, he highlighted several frequently repeated numbers. "Got a few numbers here that she called repeatedly over the last month. I'll run these through our database, see if any pop out."

Meanwhile, Sarah was examining Eleanor's financial records. "No major transactions that stand out. But she did make several small payments to a local number—it's a private entity, not a business. Could be anything from a therapist to a personal trainer."

Ian paused in his work, considering. "Or someone who knew enough about her to manipulate the situation. Let's get a name and address for that number."

Their conversation was interrupted by a knock on their cubicle wall. It was Officer Reynolds, holding a stack of files. "Hey, you two, Chief wants you to have these interview transcripts from Eleanor's colleagues and friends. Might be useful."

"Thanks, Jim," Sarah said, taking the stack and flipping through it quickly. "Let's see if anyone corroborates this change in behavior or noticed anything unusual."

They divided the stack, each taking half. Ian picked up a transcript, reading the statement from a fellow teacher at Willow's End High School. "Listen to this," he said after a minute, "One of her colleagues mentioned that Eleanor seemed anxious after attending some kind of meeting three weeks ago. Said she wasn't herself afterward."

"That aligns with the change in her social media posts," Sarah noted, looking over her shoulder. "Did they say what the meeting was about?"

"No details, just that it was some community group she was involved with recently. We need to find out more about this group."

Sarah nodded, making a note. "I'll follow up with this colleague, see if I can get more specifics. Maybe attend one of these meetings, if they're still happening."

As they continued to sift through the information, piecing together Eleanor's last weeks, the pieces of the puzzle began to form a clearer picture, though the image was still incomplete. Every email, every post, and every transaction added layers to their understanding of Eleanor, a woman who had seemingly lived an ordinary life until recently.

"Ian, check this out," Sarah said, pulling up a group photo on Eleanor's social media page. "This was taken at one of the community meetings she attended. Maybe someone here looks familiar or shows up in our other investigations."

Ian came around to her desk, examining the photo closely. "I'll run facial recognition through our database. See if any of these faces have priors or if they appear in other cases."

As they dove deeper into Eleanor's life, the shadows around her death grew denser. Each discovery, each piece of data added weight to their growing suspicion that her death was more than just a staged suicide—it was a meticulously crafted murder designed to silence whatever Eleanor had become involved with.

Focused and undeterred, Ian and Sarah prepared to follow the trail wherever it led, knowing that the answers they sought were buried in the life Eleanor had left behind. The clues were there, scattered like breadcrumbs, and it was up to them to piece it all together.

In the subdued light of the afternoon, the precinct's briefing room was tense with the presence of Chief Raymond Harte and several senior detectives. Ian and Sarah, having gathered substantial preliminary evidence, were ready to present their findings, aware that the direction they proposed might not sit well with everyone.

As the rest of the team settled, Chief Harte initiated the meeting. "Mercer, Langley, what do we have? Let's make this quick."

Ian stood, clicking the remote to bring up a presentation on the screen behind him. "Chief, based on what we've uncovered, we believe Eleanor White's death was not only a homicide but part of something bigger. Her involvement with a local community group appears more significant than initially suspected."

Sarah added, "We've traced her last few weeks of communications and financial transactions. There's a pattern of contact with certain individuals that coincides with noticeable changes in her behavior and emotional state."

One of the senior detectives, a gruff man named Detective Barnes, crossed his arms. "You're basing this on changes in her behavior and some phone calls? That seems thin."

Ian acknowledged the concern. "It's not just behavioral changes. We have forensic evidence of a struggle, and her interactions suggest she was increasingly distressed about something. Plus, we have this." He clicked to a slide showing the photo with the community group.

Sarah continued, "We believe someone in this group may have been manipulating her, possibly threatening her. We're still digging into the identities and backgrounds of these individuals."

Chief Harte rubbed his chin, considering. "And you think this community group is involved in criminal activities?"

"Yes, sir. We suspect that they might be using their cover as a community service group to conduct illegal activities. Eleanor's deepening involvement and subsequent murder could mean she discovered something she wasn't supposed to," Ian explained.

Detective Barnes scoffed. "That's a serious accusation to make based on circumstantial evidence. You're suggesting an investigation into a community group based on what—some hunches and a troubled woman?"

Sarah, sensing the rising skepticism, interjected, "Not just hunches, Detective Barnes. We have corroborating testimonies about her fear and anxiety after the meetings. And the fabric found under the bridge with someone else's blood? That's physical evidence linked to an altercation."

"Let's not forget the nature of her death. It was staged to look like a suicide," Ian added, his tone firm, meeting Barnes's gaze. "Someone wanted it to appear as a desperate act when in reality, it was orchestrated."

Chief Harte held up a hand, signaling for silence. "I appreciate your work on this, Mercer, Langley. It's clear you both believe there's more to this case. However, Detective Barnes has a point. Before we proceed with any accusations or deeper investigations into the community group, I need concrete evidence. We must tread carefully to avoid any backlash or unnecessary panic."

Ian knew the importance of the Chief's caution but also felt the urgency of the situation. "Understood, Chief. We'll continue to gather more concrete evidence. We believe the truth is just beneath the surface, and with a bit more digging, we can bring it to light."

Sarah nodded in agreement, adding, "We'll double our efforts on the forensic analysis and dig deeper into the group's activities. We're close to making a breakthrough."

As the meeting disbanded, the feeling of isolation grew stronger for Ian and Sarah. Their path was clear, yet fraught with challenges, both from within their ranks and from the shadows in which their suspects operated.

Returning to their desks, the air between them was charged with a renewed sense of purpose. "We're on the right track, Sarah. Let's prove it," Ian said quietly.

"Absolutely," Sarah replied, her eyes reflecting a steely determination. "Let's get back to it."

The precinct hummed around them, a hive of activity oblivious to the undercurrents of doubt and isolation that Ian and Sarah now navigated. But within this challenge lay the promise of uncovering the truth, a promise they intended to keep, no matter the resistance they would face.

The day was waning into evening as Detective Ian Mercer and Detective Sarah Langley continued their meticulous examination of Eleanor White's connections and the secretive community group she had been involved with. The precinct was quieter now, the bustling energy of the daytime shift giving way to the more subdued tone of the night crew.

As Ian reviewed the latest reports from the forensic team, Sarah walked over to his desk with her laptop open. "Ian, you need to see this," she said, a note of excitement breaking through her typically composed demeanor.

"What have you got?" Ian asked, leaning forward.

"I was going through the financials again, and I found a series of payments Eleanor made to a consultancy firm that doesn't seem to exist. No records of it beyond these transactions," Sarah explained, showing him the screen where transactions were highlighted.

Ian rubbed his chin thoughtfully. "That could be a front. Have you traced the account where the payments were sent?"

"That's the breakthrough," Sarah replied with a satisfied grin. "It took a bit of digging, but I traced the account to a known associate of Dr. Adrian Wolfe—our charismatic psychologist who's also part of that community group."

Ian's eyes widened. "Wolfe? This is the first solid connection we have between him and Eleanor. This could be the leverage we need to bring him in for questioning."

Sarah nodded, her fingers flying over the keyboard as she pulled up more information. "There's more. Wolfe's been under suspicion before for unethical practices, but nothing ever stuck. If we can link him to this fake consultancy, along with Eleanor's payments, we might be able to uncover more about what's really going on."

Ian stood up, his energy renewed by the breakthrough. "Good work, Sarah. Let's prepare a search warrant for Wolfe's office and home. If we're lucky, we'll find documentation linking him directly to Eleanor and possibly to other illegal activities."

"Do you think he could be the mastermind behind the staging of her death?" Sarah asked, her tone serious as she considered the implications.

"It's too early to say for sure, but I wouldn't put it past him. If he felt threatened by Eleanor possibly exposing him, he might have taken extreme measures," Ian speculated, his mind racing with possibilities.

As Ian and Sarah prepared the paperwork for the warrant, they discussed their next steps. "We need to keep this close to the chest. Wolfe is influential and has connections that could tip him off," Ian instructed, a strategic edge to his voice.

"Agreed. I'll handle the warrant application personally. We should have everything ready to go first thing in the morning," Sarah confirmed, her demeanor all business.

With their plan set, Ian glanced at his watch, realizing how late it had gotten. "Let's call it a night. We need to be sharp for tomorrow."

Sarah nodded, closing her laptop with a decisive click. "Right. See you in the morning, Ian."

As they left the precinct, the weight of their discovery hung between them, a silent acknowledgment of the dangerous path they were about to tread. But beneath that weight was a thread of anticipation—tomorrow could be the day they exposed the murky underbelly of Willow's End's seemingly serene community.

The night settled over the town, the streets quiet and watchful, mirroring the cautious steps Ian and Sarah would need to navigate in the coming days. Their first significant breakthrough in the case not only deepened the mystery but also solidified their resolve to see justice done, no matter the darkness they would have to confront.

Chapter 3
Closer Look

The early morning light filtered through the blinds of the Willow's End Police Department, casting long shadows across the worn tiles of the squad room. Detective Ian Mercer sat at his desk surrounded by files and papers, a large map of the town spread out before him, dotted with colored pins and strings that traced Eleanor White's last known movements and connections.

Detective Sarah Langley joined him, coffee in hand, placing a thick folder on the desk. "Morning, Ian. I got the warrant for Wolfe's places. We're set to go as soon as you are."

Ian nodded, his eyes not leaving the map. "Good. Let's hope this turns up something we can use." He pointed to a cluster of pins on the map. "These are all the locations associated with Wolfe, and here are the places Eleanor was last seen. I want to make sure we cover everything."

Sarah sipped her coffee, scanning the map. "I've arranged for two teams. One will handle Wolfe's office, and the other his home. We'll need to coordinate closely to ensure we don't tip him off before we can secure both locations."

As they discussed their plan, Officer Reynolds approached with a phone in hand. "Detectives, you have a call on line two. It's the lab with results from the fabric analysis."

Ian picked up the receiver, "Mercer here."

The lab technician's voice was clear and concise. "Detective, we've completed the analysis of the fabric and blood samples you sent over. The blood matches Eleanor White, and the fabric is from a shirt sold in a local boutique—fairly exclusive. We traced the purchase back to a credit card in Dr. Adrian Wolfe's name."

"Thank you, that's exactly what we needed." Ian hung up, turning to Sarah with a grim expression. "It's Wolfe's shirt. That ties him directly to the scene."

Sarah exhaled slowly. "That's a solid link. Makes our search today even more critical. We need to find anything that might suggest he was planning this, or any evidence of premeditation."

"Right. Let's get moving. We can't afford to lose any time," Ian said, gathering the files and heading towards the door.

In the car, as they drove towards Wolfe's office, the silence was filled with the soft murmur of the police radio. Sarah broke the quiet, "You think we'll find anything outright incriminating?"

Ian glanced at her, his expression thoughtful. "I hope so. But even if we don't find a smoking gun, any correspondence, documents, or even his personal effects might give us more insight into his relationship with Eleanor."

As they pulled up to Wolfe's psychology clinic, a renovated Victorian house that now served as his office, the team was already in place, waiting for their signal.

Ian checked his watch and nodded to Sarah, "Let's do this. Remember, we need to be thorough but quick. Search for any financial records, communications, anything out of the ordinary."

The team moved efficiently, each member aware of their role. Sarah directed two officers to the file room while she and Ian headed to Wolfe's personal office.

Inside, Ian went straight to the desk, rifling through drawers and examining papers. Sarah focused on the bookshelves, pulling down volumes that seemed out of place, looking for hidden compartments.

After several minutes of searching, Sarah's voice called out softly, "Ian, come here."

He joined her at the bookshelf where she was standing with a ledger in her hand. "Found this tucked away behind some old psychology texts. It's a ledger, looks like it contains records of payments received and names, lots of initials."

Ian took the ledger, flipping through it. "This could be exactly what we need. These could be payments for his... services. Let's get this back to the station and see if we can match these initials with known associates or clients."

As they left the clinic with the ledger secured, the weight of their discovery hung between them. It was a substantial find, potentially a key piece in understanding the full scope of Wolfe's dealings and his possible motivations for murder.

Back in the car, as they headed to Wolfe's residence, the morning's success was tempered by the knowledge that they were only just beginning to unravel the complex web surrounding Eleanor White's death. With each piece of evidence, the picture grew clearer, but the shadows it cast seemed only to deepen.

In the quiet privacy of the Willow's End Police Department's interrogation room, Detective Ian Mercer and Detective Sarah Langley sat across from one of Eleanor White's closest friends, Melissa Carter. Melissa, a fellow teacher at the local high school, appeared nervous but willing to help, her hands tightly clasped on the table in front of her.

Sarah began gently, "Melissa, thank you for coming in. We understand this is a difficult time, but anything you can share about Eleanor could be crucial."

Melissa nodded, her voice soft. "I'll do whatever I can to help. Eleanor was a wonderful person. It's just so hard to believe what's happened."

Ian leaned forward slightly, his tone empathetic yet firm. "We've been trying to piece together the last few weeks of Eleanor's life. Did you notice any changes in her behavior or any new stresses she might have been dealing with?"

"Yes, actually," Melissa hesitated, then continued, "Eleanor seemed distracted and... anxious lately. More so after she started attending those meetings with the new community group she found."

Sarah tilted her head, taking notes. "Can you tell us more about this group?"

Melissa sighed, "I don't know much about them, really. Eleanor was excited at first, said it was about self-improvement and connecting with influential people who could make a difference in the community. But then, she started acting like she was worried all the time, even paranoid."

Ian exchanged a glance with Sarah before asking, "Did she ever mention anyone from the group specifically? Maybe someone who might have had a bad influence?"

"There was one person she mentioned a few times... Dr. Adrian Wolfe," Melissa said, a trace of concern in her voice. "She was impressed by him initially, but then she seemed scared of him. She mentioned he was very persuasive, almost too persuasive."

Sarah's eyebrows raised slightly. "Did she ever say what made her scared?"

Melissa shook her head, "She didn't go into details. Just that she felt she was getting in over her head with something she couldn't get out of. It was unlike her to be so vague; Eleanor was usually an open book."

Ian noted this carefully. "And how about her personal life? Any new relationships or changes at home?"

"Nothing new that I knew of," Melissa replied. "Eleanor had been single for a while. She was focused on her career and this new group. It consumed a lot of her time."

As the interview concluded, Sarah reassured Melissa, "Thank you for your insights, Melissa. You've been very helpful. We're doing everything we can to get to the bottom of this."

After Melissa left, Ian and Sarah reviewed their notes. "The influence of Wolfe and this group is becoming a recurring theme," Ian observed, his voice laced with concern. "It's clear they play a significant role in whatever was troubling Eleanor."

Sarah nodded in agreement. "We need to delve deeper into Wolfe's activities and this group's members. If Eleanor was afraid, it's likely others might be as well. We should look into all the group's activities— public and private."

Ian stood, stretching slightly. "Let's pull the records of all known members and see if any patterns emerge. Financial, personal, professional—anything that can tell us more about how they operate and who else might be at risk."

As the day progressed, the pieces of Eleanor's personal life began to form a clearer picture of a woman increasingly entangled in a network that she couldn't escape. Each piece of information added a layer of complexity to their investigation, pushing Ian and Sarah to look not only at the events leading up to her death but also at the broader implications of the group's influence within Willow's End.

Late in the evening, Detective Ian Mercer found himself alone in his office, surrounded by the quiet hum of the empty precinct. The only light came from his desk lamp, casting a warm glow over the scattered papers and files that held the tangled threads of Eleanor White's life. He leaned back in his chair, the weight of the day's discoveries pressing heavily on his shoulders.

The door creaked softly as Detective Sarah Langley stepped in, her presence a welcome break in the solitude. She held two cups of coffee, offering one to Ian as she sat down across from him.

"I thought you might need this," she said, setting the cup down.

"Thanks, Sarah," Ian replied, taking a grateful sip of the hot drink. "It's been a long day."

Sarah nodded, her eyes reflecting the fatigue they both felt. "Any new insights from going over everything again?"

Ian sighed, gesturing to the files on his desk. "It's all more complex than we initially thought. Every piece of evidence seems to open up a dozen new questions. This group, their influence, it's like a web stretching across the entire town."

"And Wolfe?" Sarah inquired, leaning forward slightly.

"He's at the center of it all, it seems," Ian confirmed. "But proving it, getting enough to bring him in... it's proving more difficult than I anticipated. We need a breakthrough, something concrete."

Sarah sipped her coffee, her gaze thoughtful. "We keep digging. There's something we're missing, a connection we haven't made yet. Eleanor was scared for a reason. She knew something."

Ian nodded, his expression determined. "I keep thinking about what Melissa said, how Eleanor changed after joining that group. There's a piece of the puzzle in that transformation, something pivotal."

The room fell silent for a moment, the two detectives lost in their thoughts. It was Sarah who broke the silence. "You ever think about how cases like this change us? How we see the world?"

Ian looked at her, his eyes tired but resolute. "All the time. It's hard not to let it get to you, especially when you see the worst side of people, what they're capable of."

Sarah nodded, understanding. "But then, there are moments, breakthroughs that remind us why we do this. We're going to solve this, Ian. We'll find the truth."

Ian smiled faintly, appreciating her unwavering support. "You're right. We owe it to Eleanor and to everyone else this group might be manipulating or threatening. We need to expose them for what they are."

The conversation dwindled as they both turned their attention back to the files, the documents whispering secrets in the silence of the room. They worked well into the night, piecing together the complex narrative, each new shred of evidence adding clarity to the murky waters of the case.

As Sarah finally stood to leave, she paused at the door. "Get some rest, Ian. Tomorrow's another day, and we'll crack this. Together."

Ian watched her go, then turned back to the window, looking out over the quiet town. The streets were dark, the peaceful facades of the houses hiding the undercurrents of fear and manipulation that they were slowly uncovering. He felt the solitude of the night wrap around him, a temporary cocoon from the chaos of the investigation.

But even in this moment of reflection, his mind raced forward, chasing shadows and seeking light in the darkness of human motives. The night was deep, but the dawn was coming, and with it, the promise of new revelations.

The next morning brought a surprising development. Detective Ian Mercer was at his desk, deeply engrossed in a compilation of financial records linked to Dr. Adrian Wolfe, when Detective Sarah Langley approached with an unexpected guest in tow.

"Ian, this is Evelyn Sharp," Sarah introduced. "She was a part of the community group we've been investigating. She came forward this morning wanting to talk."

Evelyn, a woman in her early forties with a cautious but determined look, extended her hand to Ian, who stood to greet her. "Detective Mercer, I've heard you're looking into Adrian Wolfe and his... activities."

Ian nodded, motioning for her to take a seat. "Yes, we are. We believe he may be involved in some serious crimes. Anything you could tell us would be incredibly helpful."

Evelyn sat, her hands folded neatly in her lap. "I understand the risks, but I can't just watch from the sidelines anymore. What he's doing... what we were all part of, it's wrong. I want to help you bring him down."

Sarah, who had been quietly observing, spoke up, "What exactly were you involved in, Evelyn? What kind of activities are we talking about?"

Evelyn sighed, her voice a mix of fear and resolve. "It started as a group focused on empowerment, on making influential connections. But Adrian... he has a way of twisting things. He started pushing us to do things, to manipulate people, all under the guise of testing human behavior. He believes he can control fate."

Ian leaned forward, intrigued. "Can you give us specifics? Anything that shows his methods or any particular incidents that stand out?"

Evelyn nodded, her expression grim. "There were 'experiments,' as he called them. He would choose a target, someone from the town, and then he'd assign tasks to members of the group to influence that person's decisions, to push them toward a predetermined outcome."

Sarah quickly took notes, then asked, "Did Eleanor White become one of these targets?"

"Yes," Evelyn confirmed, her voice barely above a whisper. "She was the latest. I believe she realized what was happening and wanted to get out, but by then, it was too late. Adrian doesn't let go easily."

Ian's resolve hardened. "Do you have any documents, any evidence that could help us prove this in court?"

"I do," Evelyn replied, pulling a USB drive from her purse. "Emails, recordings of meetings, plans for some of the experiments. I gathered as much as I could before I left."

Sarah took the USB drive, her eyes conveying gratitude. "This is exactly what we need. Thank you, Evelyn."

Evelyn managed a small smile, though the worry was evident in her eyes. "Just... be careful. Adrian is dangerous, and he's very good at what he does."

"We will be," Ian assured her. "And we'll make sure you're protected as well."

As Evelyn left the precinct, Ian and Sarah prepared to review the contents of the USB drive. "Looks like we've just formed an unexpected alliance," Ian remarked, his tone a mixture of relief and anticipation.

"Yeah," Sarah agreed, her gaze fixed on the small piece of plastic that held so much potential. "Let's see what secrets it reveals."

They spent the rest of the day in Ian's office, poring over the files Evelyn had provided. Each document, each recording added depth to their understanding of Wolfe's manipulation and his disturbing influence over his followers.

"This is big, Sarah," Ian said as they paused for a moment, overwhelmed by the scale of the conspiracy they were uncovering. "It's not just about Eleanor anymore. It's about stopping someone who thinks he can control lives as if they're just pieces on a chessboard."

Sarah nodded, her expression steely. "Let's bring him down, Ian. For Eleanor, for all his victims."

The day wound down with both detectives more determined than ever. As the evidence laid bare the depth of Wolfe's depravity, their alliance with Evelyn not only felt right—it felt like the turning point in their fight for justice. The case was complex, the dangers real, but the path forward was clear. Together, they would dismantle Wolfe's manipulative empire, one piece of evidence at a time.

Chapter 4
Unexpected Alliance

As the morning light filtered through the blinds of the Willow's End Police Department, Detectives Ian Mercer and Sarah Langley convened in a small, stark conference room to strategize their next moves. They were joined by Chief Raymond Harte and several key members of the investigative team, each chosen for their expertise and discretion.

Ian began, organizing his notes before him on the table. "Thank you all for coming on such short notice. We have a unique situation that requires a coordinated team effort, involving complexities that go beyond typical investigations."

Chief Harte nodded, signaling Ian to continue. "Let's hear the plan, Mercer."

Ian exchanged a glance with Sarah, who then took the lead. "Based on the evidence provided by Evelyn Sharp and our ongoing investigations, we've identified several key figures in the community who are potentially involved with Adrian Wolfe's manipulative activities. Our goal is to dismantle this network and prevent further harm."

Chief Harte leaned forward, his hands clasped together. "Who are we talking about here?"

"We have a list of individuals who attended the same meetings as Eleanor and were mentioned in the documents Evelyn provided," Sarah explained, passing out copies of the list to those seated around the table. "These people range from local business owners to public servants who might be using their influence to further Wolfe's agenda."

Ian continued, "Our plan is to form two teams. One will focus on gathering more evidence, conducting interviews, and keeping tabs on the suspects' activities. The other team will handle the legal and procedural aspects, ensuring that when we make our move, it's watertight."

Detective Jameson, a seasoned investigator known for his meticulous approach, raised a question. "What about Wolfe himself? Are we bringing him in for questioning?"

"That's part of the strategy," Ian responded. "We need to approach this carefully. Wolfe is charismatic and has a significant influence. We don't want to tip him off before we have enough to hold him."

Sarah added, "Which is why our first team will also work on intercepting any communication between Wolfe and his network. We suspect they might start covering their tracks once they feel the pressure."

Detective Liu, skilled in tech and surveillance, chimed in. "I can set up monitoring on their digital footprints. Emails, social media, phone calls—anything that can give us an edge."

Chief Harte gave a firm nod. "Good. I want daily updates from both teams. Mercer, Langley, you two are in charge. Make sure everything is by the book. We can't afford any slip-ups."

Ian looked around the room, meeting the eyes of his team members. "This is more than just solving a crime. It's about protecting our community from manipulation and fear. We all need to be on top of our game."

As the meeting concluded, the team members dispersed, each with their assignments clear in their minds. Ian and Sarah lingered to discuss their immediate next steps.

"Sarah, let's prioritize the surveillance and gather as much actionable intelligence as we can in the next 48 hours," Ian suggested, his tone serious but optimistic.

Sarah nodded in agreement, her demeanor resolute. "I'll coordinate with Liu on setting up the surveillance and check in with the legal team about the warrants we might need going forward."

Their conversation was pragmatic and focused, each knowing the gravity of the task ahead. As they left the conference room, their steps were determined, their resolve echoing in the quiet halls of the precinct.

The formation of the team marked a new phase in the investigation, one that promised challenges but also the hope of finally bringing justice to those harmed by the deceptive games played by Wolfe and his associates. With the team's skills combined, Ian and Sarah felt prepared to face whatever complexities lay ahead, knowing that the strength of their collective effort was their greatest asset.

In the tech room of the Willow's End Police Department, Detective Sarah Langley and Detective Liu were huddled over multiple monitors, each displaying streams of data, social media profiles, and email threads linked to Adrian Wolfe and his known associates.

"This pattern is becoming clearer," Detective Liu noted, pointing to a timeline graph on one of the screens. "Look at the dates of these transactions and communications—they coincide with major events and decisions in our town's council over the past year."

Sarah, examining the evidence, responded thoughtfully, "So, Wolfe and his group didn't just manipulate individuals for their experiments; they tried to sway public policy too. This gives us a new angle for the investigation."

Liu clicked through another series of emails. "And there's more. See this email chain? It's between Wolfe and one of the local council members. They discuss the upcoming community center project and Wolfe's interest in influencing its planning."

Sarah leaned in closer, scrutinizing the words. "We need to document every piece of this. Can you pull up any related financial transactions or donations? Anything that shows Wolfe's influence in cash terms?"

"Already on it," Liu replied, typing rapidly. "Here we go. Wolfe's foundation made several large donations to the community project, all timed just before key decisions were made by the council."

As they continued to piece together the data, the phone rang. Sarah answered, "Langley here."

It was Ian, checking in from the field. "Sarah, how's it going in there? Finding anything that can help us tighten the noose?"

"We're uncovering a lot of coordinated activities between Wolfe and several influential figures in town. It's not just isolated incidents; it's systematic," Sarah explained, updating Ian on their findings.

"That fits with what we're seeing out here," Ian said. "We've spoken to a few people who felt pressured by Wolfe's group, not just socially but in their business dealings too. It's all adding up."

"Do you think this will be enough to get more warrants?" Sarah asked, her tone hopeful yet cautious.

"It should be," Ian responded confidently. "Keep digging and send me everything you have. I'm meeting with the DA this afternoon to discuss our next steps."

"Will do," Sarah confirmed, hanging up and turning back to Liu. "Let's compile a report with all the patterns and evidence. Ian needs it for the DA."

Liu nodded, already pulling up document templates on his computer. "I'll make sure it's detailed and clear. The connections between Wolfe's financial influence and the council's decisions are key."

As they worked, Sarah thought aloud, "It's incredible how deep this goes. Wolfe didn't just manipulate people for psychological experiments; he aimed to control the town's very fabric."

"Power corrupts," Liu remarked, half to himself. "And Wolfe had a vision for how everything should be, according to his twisted philosophy."

The room was filled with the soft clicks of keyboards and the whirring of computers as the pair documented their findings. The pattern of influence and manipulation that emerged was chilling, painting a picture of a community under the covert control of a sociopathic puppet master.

Once the report was ready, Sarah took a moment to review it. The evidence was compelling, neatly organized, and undeniably damning. "This is going to shake the town," she said, not just stating a fact, but preparing herself for the impact of their work.

Liu, finishing up the last of the attachments, replied, "Better to shake it now and root out the rot than let it fester. What you and Ian are doing—it's important, Sarah."

With the report sent to Ian, Sarah and Liu sat back, their part done for the moment, yet aware that the real challenge was just beginning. The investigation was deepening, and with each discovered pattern, the stakes grew higher and the web of deceit more tangled.

With the detailed report in hand and a clearer picture of the network they were dealing with, Detectives Ian Mercer and Sarah Langley set out to gather more tangible evidence. Their first stop was a local bookstore that, according to their intelligence, hosted several of the community group's covert meetings in a discreet back room.

As they approached the quaint, somewhat aged bookstore nestled on Main Street, the bell above the door jingled softly, announcing their arrival. The musty smell of old paper and the sight of shelves packed with books gave the place a cozy, if slightly cluttered, charm.

The owner, a middle-aged woman named Mrs. Thorton, greeted them warmly. "Welcome to Thorton's Books. How can I help you today?" she asked, her eyes flicking briefly to the badges clipped to their belts.

"Good morning, Mrs. Thorton. We're investigating a group that we believe has held meetings here. Could we have a look at the room they used?" Ian asked, his tone polite but firm.

Mrs. Thorton hesitated for a moment, then sighed, nodding. "Yes, I suppose. Follow me." She led them through the maze of bookshelves to a narrow door at the back of the shop. "They rented this room for meetings occasionally. Said it was for a book club, but they never bought books. I always thought that was odd."

As they entered the small room, Sarah looked around, noting the setup. A large table with chairs around it, a small chalkboard on one wall, and not much else. "Did you ever overhear anything unusual during these meetings?"

"Not much. They kept their voices down. Just... once I heard them talking about making sure they were persuasive enough to get someone to agree with some plan. It struck me as more intense than your usual book club discussions," Mrs. Thorton replied, wrapping her arms around herself as if chilled by the memory.

Ian photographed the room while Sarah jotted down notes. "And did you see anyone from these meetings outside of the bookstore? In town, perhaps?" Ian inquired.

"Oh, I've seen a few around, certainly. Dr. Wolfe, for one. He's hard to miss, always so charismatic. He was here for most of the meetings," she answered, her tone a mix of respect and wariness.

After thanking Mrs. Thorton, Ian and Sarah stepped outside, pausing to discuss their next steps. "We need to keep an eye on this place, see if the meetings resume, especially now that we're closing in," Sarah suggested, scanning the street thoughtfully.

"Agreed. I'll arrange for surveillance. Let's also cross-reference the names Mrs. Thorton mentioned with those we have on file. Anyone who attended these meetings could be a potential witness—or suspect," Ian added, his gaze lingering on the bookstore's old, faded sign.

The day concluded back at the station where Ian and Sarah shared a quiet moment of reflection over their findings. This initial field investigation had provided valuable insights and confirmed some of their suspicions about the group's operations.

"This is just the beginning, Sarah. The more we uncover, the deeper we see how much this group has entangled itself in the community," Ian remarked, his voice tinged with both determination and concern.

Sarah nodded, her eyes resolute. "And we'll untangle it, piece by piece. Wolfe and his group have manipulated too many lives. It's time to expose them for what they really are."

With the shadows of the bookstore investigation casting a long reach, Ian and Sarah prepared for the challenging path ahead, aware that with each step, the web of deceit they were unraveling would fight back with equal force. But their commitment to the truth was unwavering, driven by the knowledge that behind every deceptive facade lay the stories of real victims, waiting for justice.

As dusk fell over Willow's End, Detectives Ian Mercer and Sarah Langley found themselves once again in the quiet confines of their office at the police station, pouring over the day's accumulations of interviews, surveillance data, and Mrs. Thorton's hesitant yet revealing testimony.

"I think we're finally getting to the core of Wolfe's operations," Ian said, spreading out a map of the town on the table. The map was dotted with various markers, each representing key locations tied to Wolfe and his group. "These spots here, the bookstore, his clinic, and a couple of these other meeting places—it's like he's created a circuit, a loop of influence."

Sarah, who had been organizing the evidence files, looked up, her eyes scanning the map. "And with each spot, he's been able to weave this network tighter around the community. It's strategic, methodical. This isn't just about random manipulation; it's orchestrated control."

Ian nodded, his expression grave. "Which is why our next steps are crucial. We need to anticipate his moves. Based on the patterns we've seen, where do you think he'll strike next?"

Sarah leaned over the map, tracing a line with her finger from the bookstore to a nearby community center. "Here. They've had meetings here before, and with the community center's new program launch next week, it would be a perfect cover for him to gather his group, under the guise of public service."

"That makes sense," Ian agreed, making a note. "We'll need to set up surveillance at the community center then. Discreet, though. The last thing we want is to spook him before we gather enough evidence for an arrest."

"Exactly. And I've been thinking about Evelyn's role in all of this," Sarah added, her tone cautious. "She's given us valuable intel, but Wolfe might still see her as a threat, a loose end. We should consider protective surveillance for her too."

Ian considered this, rubbing his chin thoughtfully. "Agreed. Let's arrange that. Her safety is a priority, especially since she's come forward to help us."

The room was silent for a moment, both detectives deep in thought, until Ian broke the quiet. "Sarah, I want to acknowledge the work you've been doing here. This case... it's one of the toughest we've faced, and I couldn't have asked for a better partner in this."

Sarah smiled slightly, appreciating the sentiment. "Thanks, Ian. I feel the same. We make a good team. And we'll crack this case, together."

Ian smiled back, then glanced again at the map. "Tomorrow, I'll touch base with the surveillance team to update them on these plans. We'll need eyes on that community center event, and possibly on some of the other locations on this map as the event draws closer."

"Meanwhile, I'll continue to dig into the financial trails. There's more to uncover about how Wolfe's funding all this, and who else might be involved financially," Sarah said, her mind already racing with the possibilities of what they might find.

"Perfect. Let's reconvene first thing in the morning to see where we stand and finalize the details," Ian concluded, starting to gather the papers and prepare to leave for the night.

As they packed up, the weight of their responsibility lingered in the air, a silent testament to the gravity of their investigation. The trust and reliance they placed in each other had grown stronger with each passing day, each discovery leading them further into the depths of Wolfe's deceptive schemes.

With the strategy set and their roles clearly defined, Ian and Sarah left the station, the town around them quiet under the night sky, unaware of the storm that was brewing just beneath its serene surface. The next few days would be critical, and as they drove away from the precinct, both detectives felt the anticipation of the impending confrontation with Wolfe and his network—a confrontation that would undoubtedly test their skills and their newly fortified partnership.

Chapter 5
Shadows of the Past

In the dim light of Ian Mercer's office, the air hung heavy with anticipation. Detective Sarah Langley and Detective Ian Mercer had convened to delve deeper into the origins and motivations of Dr. Adrian Wolfe, which seemed to be at the heart of their investigation. They were joined by Evelyn Sharp, whose intimate knowledge of Wolfe and his manipulations had proven invaluable.

Ian, with a stack of old newspaper clippings and various psychological profiles scattered across his desk, initiated the conversation. "Understanding Wolfe's background could give us insight into his motivations. Evelyn, you mentioned before that Wolfe had a particularly influential childhood. Can you elaborate on that?"

Evelyn nodded, her hands clasped tightly in her lap, a sign of the tension she felt revisiting the topic. "Yes, Adrian often spoke about his upbringing during the group sessions. He was raised by a father who was a renowned psychologist himself. From what Adrian described, his father was domineering, used his knowledge to manipulate those around him—including Adrian."

Sarah, taking notes, interjected, "So, he grew up in an environment where psychological manipulation was normalized?"

"Exactly," Evelyn continued. "Adrian admired and resented his father in equal measure. He inherited his father's charisma and insight into human psychology but used those skills to test his theories about control and manipulation."

Ian, deep in thought, added, "So his actions now might be an extension of that—pushing boundaries to see how much he can control others?"

"Precisely," Evelyn confirmed. "It's like he's playing out his childhood dynamics on a larger scale, trying to prove he's better than his father ever was."

Sarah, looking up from her notes, suggested, "We need to pull up more on his father's background. There might be past colleagues or case studies that can shed light on the psychological methods that influenced Adrian."

"I'll get on that," Ian said, pulling his laptop closer. "Meanwhile, Evelyn, was there a specific event or turning point for Adrian that escalated his behavior?"

Evelyn sighed, a distant look in her eyes. "There was an incident during his late teens—his mother, who was the only person he seemed to genuinely care about, left his father. Adrian was devastated. He believed his father's manipulative traits drove her away. It hardened him, made him obsessed with understanding and mastering manipulation."

Ian typed quickly, searching for public records on the incident. "This could explain his drive to dominate others, to never again feel as powerless as he did when his mother left."

Sarah nodded thoughtfully. "It's a pattern of overcompensation. If we present this profile to the DA, it could help establish a motive for his current actions and his psychological state."

The team spent the next few hours compiling a detailed psychological profile of Adrian Wolfe, integrating insights from Evelyn with historical data and psychological theories that might explain his complex motivations. They explored how his past was not just a backstory but a blueprint for his current schemes.

As the meeting drew to a close, Evelyn thanked Ian and Sarah. "I never understood fully why Adrian did what he did, but talking about it now, it's clearer. It's tragic, really."

Ian stood and offered a reassuring smile. "Your insights have been invaluable, Evelyn. We're closer now than we ever were to understanding Wolfe and hopefully stopping him."

Sarah added, "Yes, thank you. We'll make sure your courage in coming forward wasn't in vain."

The detectives remained in the office long after Evelyn had left, piecing together the final parts of their report. Their conversation had revealed not just the shadows of Adrian Wolfe's past but had also cast light on the deeper, darker motives behind his actions. As they prepared to take this information to the DA, they knew they were arming themselves with more than just facts—they were bringing the psychological depth that would be crucial in understanding and countering Wolfe's manipulations.

Detective Ian Mercer and Detective Sarah Langley sat in the stark, fluorescent-lit room of the Willow's End Police Department, pouring over new reports that had just come in. A fresh wave of urgency washed over them as they connected recent events to their ongoing investigation of Adrian Wolfe.

"Look at this, Sarah," Ian said, handing her a police report. "We have another incident. A local businessman, Tom Clarkson, was found in a state of extreme distress at his office. He's claiming he was coerced into making several risky business decisions against his better judgment."

Sarah skimmed the report, her brow furrowing. "Coerced? Does it say how or by whom?"

Ian nodded gravely. "He mentioned psychological pressure, mind games that left him confused about his own decisions. It's eerily similar to what we've seen with Wolfe's other victims. I think we need to talk to him, see if there's a direct link."

The detectives wasted no time and soon found themselves at the local hospital where Tom was under observation. They entered his room to find a middle-aged man sitting up in bed, looking weary but alert.

"Mr. Clarkson, I'm Detective Langley and this is Detective Mercer. We're investigating a series of incidents that we believe may be connected to what happened to you," Sarah began, her voice gentle yet firm.

Tom glanced between the two detectives, his expression one of mixed relief and apprehension. "I didn't think anyone would believe me. It's been... surreal. I've never felt so out of control."

Ian pulled up a chair next to the bed. "We're taking your situation very seriously, Mr. Clarkson. Can you tell us about who or what led to this feeling of losing control?"

Tom took a deep breath, steadying himself before answering. "It started a few months ago after I attended a seminar. It was led by a man named Adrian Wolfe. He was persuasive, charismatic, and I... I was drawn in by his confidence. But then, the meetings got strange."

Sarah noted this down, then asked, "Strange in what way?"

"He began suggesting risky investments, strategies that didn't make sense. But the way he presented them, and the psychological tactics he used... I started doubting my own logic," Tom explained, his voice shaky.

Ian exchanged a look with Sarah. "Did Wolfe ever threaten you, or did it feel like you were being manipulated?"

"It was manipulation, definitely. He has a way of getting into your head. I felt like I was being pulled deeper into something I couldn't escape from," Tom said, looking down at his hands.

"Thank you for sharing this, Mr. Clarkson. It's extremely important to our case," Sarah said, offering a sympathetic smile. "We believe Wolfe has done this to others. We're working to stop him."

As the detectives left the hospital, they discussed their next steps in the car. "We need to expose Wolfe's methods publicly. Clarkson's story could be the key to connecting Wolfe to these coercive tactics," Ian suggested, starting the engine.

Sarah nodded in agreement. "Let's prepare a detailed statement for the press. If we can get more victims to come forward, we can build a stronger case and prevent further harm."

"Exactly," Ian said as he drove back to the station. "And we should also check if there are financial trails linking Clarkson's investments back to Wolfe or his associates."

Their conversation continued, each detail adding to their understanding and strategy. The connection to Tom Clarkson not only reinforced the pattern of Wolfe's manipulations but also opened a new avenue for the investigation. The detectives knew that with each victim who came forward, they were not just closer to stopping Wolfe but also to understanding the full extent of his influence and control over the community.

The day closed with a resolve strengthened by the new developments, and as the shadows of the past continued to reveal themselves, Ian and Sarah prepared to shine a light so bright that not even Wolfe's manipulations could withstand it.

On a chill, overcast afternoon, Detective Ian Mercer and Detective Sarah Langley found themselves driving away from the bustling center of Willow's End to the more secluded, tree-lined neighborhood where Ian had grown up. The journey was not just a physical one; it was a plunge into Ian's past, prompted by their deep dive into Wolfe's background and its revelations about how the past shapes the present.

As they turned onto the familiar, narrow lane leading to Ian's childhood home, now more weathered and empty since his parents had moved away, Ian spoke up, a hint of nostalgia mixed with apprehension in his voice. "I haven't been back here since my mom passed. My dad sold it just after, said there were too many memories."

Sarah, sensing the weight of the moment, offered a supportive smile. "What was it like, growing up here?"

Ian slowed the car as they approached the old two-story house, its paint faded and garden overgrown. "It was good, mostly. Quiet. My parents were supportive, but..." He paused, searching for the right words. "My dad was a police officer, too. He was stern, had high expectations. I spent a lot of time trying to live up to them."

They parked in front of the house and got out, the crunch of gravel underfoot breaking the silence. Walking up the path, Ian continued, "He believed in tough love. Said it would make me strong, ready to face anything. I guess it did, but it also made me question my own decisions, wondering if they'd ever be good enough."

Sarah listened intently, connecting the dots. "Do you think that's why you're so driven in your work? Always digging deeper, making sure everything's right?"

Ian nodded, his gaze lingering on the front door, now slightly ajar. "Probably. I've always felt like I had something to prove, not just to him but to myself. That I could make a difference, do things right."

They stepped inside, the house still holding echoes of Ian's childhood. As they moved through the empty rooms, each corner seemed to hold a memory, a ghost of the past. Ian pointed to a corner of the living room. "I used to sit there for hours, reading, watching Dad work on cases. He'd lay out his files, tell me about the importance of justice, of protecting those who couldn't protect themselves."

Sarah, understanding more of her partner now than perhaps ever before, reflected, "It's like you took all those lessons and built your own way of dealing with the world. And it's brought you here, doing what you do."

"Yeah," Ian agreed, a faint smile crossing his face. "Though sometimes I wonder what he'd make of how I handle my cases, if he'd think I was doing the right thing."

"I think he'd be proud, Ian," Sarah said sincerely. "Proud of how you've used those lessons to become not just a good detective, but a great one. And how you're handling the Wolfe case, it's personal, but you're not letting it cloud your judgment."

Ian looked around, his eyes reflecting a mix of sorrow and resolve. "Thanks, Sarah. That means a lot."

As they left the house, the weight of Ian's past seemed to linger, yet it also felt like a chapter that was slowly closing, allowing him to focus fully on the present challenge. "Let's get back, we have a lot to prepare. Wolfe won't know what hit him," Ian said with renewed determination.

Driving back, their conversation drifted to lighter topics, but the visit had clearly deepened their partnership, a shared understanding between them that would strengthen their resolve in the battles to come. As Willow's End faded back into view, both detectives felt ready to confront whatever shadows lay ahead, armed not just with evidence and strategy, but with the profound bonds of shared histories and mutual respect.

Back at the precinct, Detectives Ian Mercer and Sarah Langley settled into the dim glow of the operations room, surrounded by the buzz of police scanners and the soft clacking of keyboards. Their recent visit to Ian's childhood home had unearthed not just personal memories but also a renewed sense of purpose. Now, as they reviewed the latest intelligence gathered on Adrian Wolfe, every piece of information seemed to echo with deeper significance.

Sarah, her eyes scanning through emails and notes on her computer screen, broke the silence. "Ian, this email chain between Wolfe and one of his main financial backers—it's revealing. They're not just talking about investments; there's a clear implication here that Wolfe is using his influence for more than just financial gain."

Ian leaned over to look at the screen. "Can you pull up that part about the new initiative he's planning?"

"Right here," Sarah pointed at a paragraph in the email. "It says, 'With the new initiative, we can reshape the community to our vision. It's time to accelerate our efforts.' It's like he's not even hiding his intentions anymore."

"That's because he's confident he's untouchable. But this," Ian tapped on the screen, "this could be the leverage we need. If we link this directly to any illegal activities, it could be enough to bring him in."

Sarah nodded in agreement, her mind racing with the legal implications. "I'll get this over to the DA. We need to make sure we have everything buttoned up legally."

As they prepared the documents, their conversation continued to weave through the implications of their findings. "Ian, how are you feeling about all this?" Sarah asked, her tone shifting to concern for her partner. "After visiting your old home, and now this... it's a lot to process."

Ian sighed, a mix of fatigue and resolve in his expression. "It's strange. Seeing where I came from, understanding why I do this—it's grounding. And it's making me even more determined to see this through. Wolfe's manipulation of this town... it's personal to me now."

"I can see that," Sarah replied, offering a supportive smile. "And you're not in this alone. We're going to see this through together."

The camaraderie and mutual respect between them were palpable as they shared a quiet moment of understanding. Then, Ian stood up, his posture firm, the detective shield back in place. "Let's go over our plan one more time. We need to ensure no stone is left unturned when we move against Wolfe."

Sarah pulled up a digital map of the town, with various locations marked. "We'll need surveillance here and here," she pointed at specific spots, "and we need to coordinate with the team on the ground to ensure we have real-time updates. Any slip-up could give Wolfe a heads-up."

Ian nodded, reviewing the map. "Right. And let's make sure the surveillance vans are unmarked and the officers know to keep a low profile. The last thing we need is to spook him."

"Exactly. I'll also set up a meeting with the other department heads. We need all hands on deck for this," Sarah added, her tone all business.

As they finalized their strategy, their resolve solidified. The room, with its maps and screens and endless flows of data, seemed to shrink around them, focusing all energy on the task at hand.

"We've got this, Sarah," Ian said as they packed up their files, ready to leave for the night. "Tomorrow, we bring him down."

Sarah nodded, her expression one of fierce determination. "Tomorrow it ends."

As they left the precinct, the weight of their impending confrontation with Wolfe loomed large. Yet, beneath that weight was a foundation of trust and shared commitment, a bond forged through challenges and solidified by the shared resolve to protect their community from the shadows that sought to control it.

Chapter 6
The Club Exposed

Under the cloak of early evening, Detectives Ian Mercer and Sarah Langley positioned themselves in an unmarked police vehicle parked across the street from an upscale, nondescript building in downtown Willow's End. This building, according to their investigation, housed the elite club where Adrian Wolfe often held his most secretive meetings.

Ian adjusted the focus on the binoculars, peering through the tinted windows of their car towards the building's entrance. "There's movement. Looks like we have some of the usual suspects arriving," he murmured, his voice low.

Sarah, next to him, kept her eyes on a laptop screen that displayed live feeds from other hidden cameras they had installed earlier around the premises. "I've got visuals on the side entrance. That's Derek Simmons, Wolfe's right-hand man. He's with someone new, could be another recruit."

"Keep an eye on that entrance. If Wolfe shows up, he might use it to avoid the main door," Ian suggested, not taking his eyes from the binoculars. "Anything unusual about the new guy's behavior?"

Sarah zoomed in on the feed, observing the newcomer. "He looks nervous, keeps checking his phone and looking around. Doesn't seem comfortable with the secrecy."

"That could work in our favor. Someone not fully indoctrinated might slip up, give us more to work with," Ian noted, scribbling something in his notepad.

As they continued their surveillance, a sleek black car pulled up to the front. "Here we go. Wolfe's just arrived," Ian said, tension lining his voice as he watched Adrian Wolfe step out, his demeanor calm and authoritative as he greeted a few familiar faces before heading inside.

Sarah switched feeds, focusing on the interior cameras they had managed to plant inside the main meeting hall. "Cameras are rolling inside. We should be able to hear most of what's said during the meeting. The audio bugs were a good call, Ian."

"Let's hope they reveal something we can use to tie Wolfe directly to the manipulations and not just vague insinuations," Ian replied, his gaze fixed on the building. "How's the recording setup? We need clean audio for the DA."

"All systems are green. We're recording everything," Sarah confirmed, checking the settings one more time.

They watched in silence as the meeting seemed to get underway, the low murmur of voices barely audible through their audio equipment. Ian's hand tightened around the binoculars when Wolfe took a central position in the room, obviously leading the gathering.

"Listen to this, Ian. Wolfe's talking about expanding their influence, mentions pushing their agenda in the next city council meeting," Sarah said, her fingers flying over the keyboard as she logged every word.

"Perfect. That's exactly the kind of evidence we need to show his intentions aren't just financial but politically coercive as well," Ian responded, a slight edge of satisfaction in his tone.

As the meeting continued, Ian and Sarah remained vigilant, documenting every participant and every piece of dialogue they could capture. The operation was risky, but as each minute passed, they gathered more evidence.

"Think we'll get enough tonight to move in?" Sarah asked after a while, her voice hopeful yet anxious.

"We'll assess at the end of the meeting. If we can catch them in a clear act of conspiracy, especially Wolfe, it might be our best chance to bring him in without tipping off the whole network," Ian calculated, his mind already on the next steps.

As the evening wore on, the detectives' collection of covert recordings grew. Each participant leaving the building looked satisfied, unaware of the detectives documenting their every move.

When the last of them had left and the building stood dark and silent, Ian and Sarah finally allowed themselves to relax back into their seats, the intensity of the operation easing off.

"We've got some solid material here, Sarah. Let's get back, go through everything thoroughly, and plan our approach with the DA," Ian suggested, starting the car.

"Agreed. Tonight was a success, but the real work starts now," Sarah said as they pulled away from the curb, the building fading into the rearview mirror.

The night's operation had deepened their case against Wolfe, adding layers of complexity to their understanding but also providing them with the tangible evidence they needed. As they drove back to the precinct, both detectives felt the weight of what was to come, knowing that the challenge ahead was daunting but necessary to protect their community from the shadows they had just exposed.

The plan to infiltrate Adrian Wolfe's next meeting was set with meticulous care. Detective Sarah Langley, under the guise of a potential new member, was to enter the meeting alongside Detective Ian Mercer, who would pose as her colleague interested in the club's community influence initiatives. Their backstory was carefully crafted, supported by fake identities and a convincing cover story.

As they approached the discreetly marked venue, a modern but unassuming building on the outskirts of Willow's End, Sarah adjusted the microphone hidden beneath her blouse, while Ian checked the small camera concealed in his tie. The air was thick with tension, the weight of their task palpable between them.

"Remember, just blend in and gather as much intel as you can. We need concrete evidence of illegal activities or direct coercion," Ian whispered as they climbed the steps to the building.

Sarah nodded, her expression calm but her nerves on edge. "Let's hope Wolfe doesn't recognize us from any of the surveillance footage."

The interior of the venue was sleek and modern, with abstract art adorning the walls and plush seating arranged in a semi-circle around a central speaking area. The attendees were a mix of well-dressed individuals, each exuding a sense of purpose and secrecy.

As they mingled, Ian and Sarah were approached by Derek Simmons, Wolfe's right-hand man. "Welcome, I don't believe we've met. I'm Derek," he said, offering a hand.

Ian shook it, introducing both himself and Sarah with their aliases. "We heard great things about the impact your group is having on the community and wanted to see it firsthand."

Derek nodded, seemingly satisfied with their explanation. "You'll find our work very rewarding. Adrian is just about to begin."

The meeting commenced with Adrian Wolfe taking the stage, his presence commanding attention. He began discussing their recent 'achievements' and future plans, his words carefully coded for those initiated, but Ian and Sarah could read between the lines.

"This community is ripe for change, a change that we can steer. With your help, we can ensure that our vision becomes the reality. It's about guiding decisions at every level," Wolfe articulated with a persuasive calmness.

Sarah, maintaining her role, asked a planted question, "Could you elaborate on what kind of decisions we might influence?"

Wolfe smiled, a glint of cunning in his eyes. "Let's just say that from local business partnerships to city council elections, we ensure the right people are in the right places. It's all about alignment."

Ian, observing the crowd's reactions, noted several nods of agreement. The implication was clear: Wolfe's network was manipulating more than just business deals; they were deep into local politics.

As the meeting broke into smaller groups, Ian and Sarah continued to engage with the attendees, gathering names and details, while their hidden devices recorded everything.

Later, as they walked back to their car, Sarah let out a deep breath. "That was intense. I think we got what we needed, though. The recordings should give us enough to go on."

Ian nodded, starting the car. "Yes, it's a relief to be out of there. Let's review everything as soon as we get back. If Wolfe's claims are as solid as they sound, this could be the break we've been waiting for."

Driving away from the venue, the evening's earlier tension slowly dissipated, replaced by a cautious optimism. Their infiltration had not only provided them with valuable insights but also confirmed the depth of Wolfe's influence.

Back at the station, they immediately began the process of reviewing the recordings, each piece of evidence further validating their mission. The night's work had deepened their understanding of Wolfe's operations and brought them one step closer to dismantling his network.

As they prepared for the next phase of their investigation, Ian and Sarah knew the challenges ahead would be formidable. Yet, with each successful operation, their resolve only strengthened, ready to face whatever Wolfe and his clandestine club might throw their way.

Following their successful infiltration of the meeting, Detectives Ian Mercer and Sarah Langley prepared for a more confrontational phase of their investigation. They knew that a direct encounter with Dr. Adrian Wolfe was inevitable and potentially dangerous. Yet, it was crucial to gather his reactions to specific allegations that could help strengthen their case against him.

The opportunity arose sooner than they expected. Information came through their network that Wolfe would be attending a public event at a local art gallery, a place he was known to frequent as a patron. The detectives decided this would be the perfect setting for a less formal but intentional encounter.

As they entered the gallery, the modern space was abuzz with the town's elite, making it a neutral ground that was public yet intimate enough for a meaningful conversation. Wolfe was already there, mingling with a group of influential figures, his charismatic presence unmistakable.

Ian nudged Sarah, and they made their approach. As they neared, Ian cleared his throat, attracting Wolfe's attention. "Dr. Wolfe, I believe? I'm Ian Mercer, and this is my colleague, Sarah Langley."

Wolfe turned, his expression one of polite interest. "Yes, I am. How can I help you?"

"We've been following your work with the community very closely," Ian began, maintaining a professional yet firm tone. "Your methods of influence are quite innovative. We are particularly interested in how you manage to guide public opinion and decisions."

Wolfe's eyes narrowed slightly, a flicker of caution passing over his features. "My methods are simply about understanding people, Detective. I'm sure you can appreciate the value of that in your line of work."

Sarah joined in, her voice calm. "Absolutely, Dr. Wolfe. However, we're curious about the extent of this influence. There are concerns that it might go beyond simple persuasion."

Wolfe smiled, a thin, practiced gesture. "Concerns? Well, influence is a tool, much like any other. It can be misinterpreted by those not familiar with its delicate handling."

Ian decided to press further, subtly hinting at their deeper knowledge. "What about when influence crosses into manipulation, especially within political circles? Where do you draw the line?"

Wolfe maintained his composure, his reply smooth as silk. "The line is drawn by the law, Detective. As long as my actions are within legal boundaries, my conscience is clear. Are you suggesting otherwise?"

"Not suggesting, Dr. Wolfe, just trying to understand the breadth of your activities," Sarah clarified, watching his reactions closely.

"The breadth of my activities is wide but always transparent, at least to those who choose to see it that way," Wolfe responded, his tone still friendly but with an edge that suggested the conversation was treading into less comfortable territory.

Ian took a slight step forward, reducing the physical and metaphorical distance. "Transparency is good, that's why we're here. To clarify, to understand. Perhaps you'd be willing to discuss your methods more openly? A formal interview at the station?"

Wolfe chuckled softly, the sound more a display of decorum than amusement. "A formal interview? I'm afraid my schedule is quite full. However, should you have any legitimate concerns, feel free to reach out through my office."

"Thank you, Dr. Wolfe. We'll certainly consider that," Sarah said, offering a polite smile that masked her true intent.

As they excused themselves and left the gallery, the brief exchange had provided them not only with insight into Wolfe's guarded nature but also with a firsthand account of his adeptness at navigating probing questions.

In the car, Ian turned to Sarah, "What do you think?"

"He's careful, very careful. But he slipped up, the way he defends his influence. There's something there, Ian. We just need to push a little harder," Sarah replied, her mind already racing with the next steps.

Their first direct encounter with Wolfe had set the stage for what would undoubtedly be a complex battle of wits and wills. As they drove back to the precinct, both detectives knew that the real confrontation was still to come, and it would require all their skills to bring Wolfe's hidden empire into the light.

As the evening waned, Detectives Ian Mercer and Sarah Langley found themselves in a precarious situation. After their encounter with Dr. Adrian Wolfe at the gallery, they felt the urgent need to delve deeper and intercept a crucial meeting believed to be the venue for Wolfe's next major strategic move. However, aware that Wolfe might now be suspicious of them, they needed to approach this with utmost caution to avoid detection.

The location was an old, somewhat rundown estate on the outskirts of Willow's End, known among the locals for its sprawling grounds and a long history of being a secluded meeting spot for various private gatherings. Under the cover of darkness, Ian and Sarah, along with a small team of trusted officers, positioned themselves strategically around the perimeter. They used night vision equipment to keep watch without making their presence known.

Ian communicated quietly through his headset, his voice barely a whisper, "Team two, report status."

"All clear on the west wing of the property. No movement detected," came the hushed reply over the radio.

Sarah, crouched low in the shadows beside Ian, kept her eyes fixed on the back entrance of the mansion. The night was eerily silent, the rustle of leaves and the occasional distant call of a night owl the only sounds breaking the stillness.

As the time for the meeting drew near, tension mounted. Ian checked his watch, the soft glow of the dial illuminating his focused expression. "They should be arriving any minute now. Keep your eyes peeled."

Minutes ticked by slowly, each second stretching longer than the last. Finally, the faint sound of multiple vehicles approached. Through the dense foliage, the lights of cars turning into the long driveway of the estate became visible. Ian signaled to Sarah, and both increased their vigilance.

The cars parked, and figures began to disembark, their features obscured by the dim lighting. Ian used a small, high-powered scope to try to identify any of the arrivals. "I see Wolfe. He's here," he confirmed softly, his voice tense.

Sarah nodded, recording the arrival time in her notes. As the group moved towards the mansion, the detectives did not dare follow too closely. Instead, they relied on the pre-placed listening devices they had managed to install inside earlier that day.

The risk of physically entering the building was too high. Wolfe was known for his paranoia and meticulous attention to security, especially during these covert gatherings. Instead, Ian and Sarah retreated to a safer distance, where they could monitor the communications coming from their devices.

Listening through the earpieces, they caught snippets of conversation about financial transactions, manipulation strategies, and even veiled references to political maneuvers planned for the coming months. Each piece of overheard dialogue was carefully logged for later analysis and use in building their case.

As the meeting continued, Ian and Sarah remained hidden in the darkness, their presence undetected by Wolfe and his associates. The night grew colder, and they huddled in their jackets, the adrenaline of the operation keeping them alert.

Finally, after what seemed like hours, the meeting concluded. The cars slowly began to filter out of the estate's driveway, disappearing down the road from which they had come. Only once the last taillights had vanished into the night did Ian and Sarah dare to move.

"Let's head back," Ian whispered, leading the way back to their own vehicle parked a safe distance away. As they drove away from the estate, both detectives felt a mix of relief and urgency.

"We got what we came for, but this is just the beginning," Sarah said, her mind already on the next steps.

Ian nodded in agreement, the road ahead lit only by their headlights. "Right. It's time to put all these pieces together and bring Wolfe and his network down. For good."

Their escape from detection had been narrow, but successful. Now, armed with new information and determined more than ever, Ian and Sarah were ready to face the challenges that awaited them in their quest to expose and dismantle the sinister operations of The Club.

Chapter 7
Philosophical Clashes

The morning sun filtered through the blinds of Detective Ian Mercer's office, casting long, striped shadows across the floor and onto the desk where he and Detective Sarah Langley were deep in discussion. They were not alone; joining them was Dr. Helen Carter, a psychologist specializing in manipulative behaviors, whom they had consulted to better understand and predict Adrian Wolfe's moves.

"So, Dr. Carter, based on what we've observed, Wolfe enjoys using psychological games to assert control. How can we use this to our advantage?" Ian asked, leaning forward, his elbows on the desk.

Dr. Carter adjusted her glasses thoughtfully. "It's classic behavior for someone who believes in their own intellectual superiority. He may use riddles or complex scenarios to challenge and dismantle his opponent's understanding. It's both a test and a trap."

Sarah, who was taking notes, looked up. "A trap in what sense?"

"In the sense that engaging with him on this level might lead you to reveal more about your own strategy than you intend to," Dr. Carter explained. "However, if you're prepared, you can turn this tactic around on him. He'll be looking for signs of confusion or weakness. If you show neither, it can unsettle him, push him to make a misstep."

Ian nodded, absorbing the insight. "So, we play along but keep it close to the vest. We'll need to be careful about what we disclose."

"Exactly," Dr. Carter affirmed. "And remember, he might pose questions or scenarios that have underlying meanings. It's important to think about what he's not saying just as much as what he is."

The conversation was interrupted by a phone call. Ian picked up, listened for a moment, and then hung up with a grim expression. "That was the station. Wolfe has just invited us to a 'friendly' public debate. He's throwing down the gauntlet, in a manner of speaking."

Sarah raised an eyebrow. "A public debate? That's risky for him. What's his angle?"

Dr. Carter offered an explanation. "It's another psychological game. He's trying to outplay you in a public arena. Wolfe is confident in his ability to manipulate a crowd. But this is also your opportunity to unsettle him, as we discussed."

Ian thought for a moment, then made a decision. "We'll accept. But we'll control the narrative. Sarah, let's prepare our topics carefully. We need to be strategic about what we bring to the table."

Sarah nodded, already brainstorming. "We could bring up topics that are indirectly related to his activities. It'll force him to navigate carefully, without making it obvious that we're probing."

"Good," Ian said. "And let's think of some riddles or complex questions of our own. If he wants to play games, we'll show him we can play, too."

Dr. Carter smiled approvingly. "Keep him on his toes, and watch for his reactions. They'll tell you a lot about his state of mind and confidence levels."

With the debate set for the next day, Ian and Sarah spent the rest of the day preparing, going over potential questions and answers, and strategizing the best ways to expose Wolfe's methods without revealing their hand. They rehearsed exchanges, with Dr. Carter providing feedback on their delivery and tactics.

As the day turned to evening, both detectives felt a cautious optimism. The upcoming debate was not just a confrontation but a crucial play in their ongoing battle of wits with Wolfe.

"This isn't just about winning a debate," Ian mused as they wrapped up their session. "It's about revealing his true nature, his manipulation. We expose him, and we weaken him."

Sarah, packing up her notes, agreed. "Tomorrow, we show that his psychological games can be turned against him. It's a chess match, and we need to think several moves ahead."

Leaving the office, the detectives felt prepared, their strategy set. The game was on, and they were ready to meet Wolfe's challenge head-on, armed with their own riddles and a deep understanding of the psychological battleground they were about to enter.

In the quiet, well-lit library of the Willow's End precinct, Detective Ian Mercer and Detective Sarah Langley sat across from each other at a large oak table strewn with books, academic papers, and their own notes. They were deep in preparation for the upcoming public debate with Adrian Wolfe, focusing particularly on the philosophical underpinnings that could be expected to influence his arguments.

Ian had selected several texts on ethics and power dynamics, his eyes scanning a passage about the philosophy of control. "Listen to this," he said, reading aloud, "'The exercise of power is legitimate only when it respects the ethical autonomy of all individuals involved.' This could be a cornerstone for challenging Wolfe's ideologies. It's all about undermining the ethical justification he may claim for his actions."

Sarah nodded, her mind absorbing the information while also analyzing its implications. "That's a solid angle, Ian. If we can argue that his manipulations compromise individual autonomy, it undercuts any moral high ground he might try to claim."

She turned to a chapter in her own book, which dealt with the philosophical concept of 'the social contract.' "Here's something," she started, pointing to a specific paragraph. "This section discusses how societal trust is foundational to the social contract. Wolfe's actions erode that trust and, by extension, damage the very fabric of the social contract."

Ian considered this, tapping his pen against the table thoughtfully. "That's good, really good. We can argue that Wolfe isn't just manipulating individuals, but he's threatening the structure of society itself."

The detectives spent the next few hours delving deeper into philosophical texts, each bringing a different perspective on power, control, and morality. They discussed and debated among themselves, sharpening their arguments, anticipating counterarguments Wolfe might use, and reinforcing their positions with philosophical citations.

As they worked, the room was filled with a heavy silence, broken only by the occasional shuffle of papers or murmur of a particularly intriguing point. The depth of their preparation was not just about winning a debate; it was about understanding the moral implications of Wolfe's actions and framing these in a way that the public could understand and resonate with.

"This Nietzsche quote could be risky, but it might work if used carefully," Ian suggested, reading from another text. "'Whoever fights monsters should see to it that in the process he does not become a monster. And if you gaze long enough into an abyss, the abyss will gaze back into you.'" He looked up at Sarah. "It's a caution about becoming what we oppose. We could use it to highlight the danger Wolfe poses, not just to others, but to himself."

Sarah weighed the idea, her expression thoughtful. "It's powerful, but you're right, it's risky. It could backfire or be seen as too philosophical. We need to make sure our audience grasitates the implications without feeling lectured."

The discussion eventually veered towards practical applications of these philosophical concepts, considering the audience's likely background and how best to communicate complex ideas in accessible ways. The goal was to make Wolfe's philosophical stance appear not only misguided but dangerous.

As they packed up their materials, the weight of their task settled around them, a mixture of determination and the sobering realization of the challenge ahead. They were not just preparing for a debate; they were preparing to expose a dangerous ideology that threatened their community.

Leaving the library, the cool evening air felt refreshing after hours spent in the warmth of intense intellectual effort. Ian glanced at Sarah, a slight smile of camaraderie on his face. "We're ready for him, aren't we?"

Sarah returned the smile, her eyes firm with resolve. "We're ready. Let's bring his philosophical house down."

They walked back to their cars, the night around them quiet, but the ideas and strategies they had honed in the library continued to resonate, ready to be deployed in the philosophical battle that awaited.

Back at the precinct after a long day of preparation, Detective Ian Mercer found himself alone in his office, the weight of their upcoming confrontation with Adrian Wolfe pressing heavily on him. The door opened, and Detective Sarah Langley stepped in, her expression mirroring the concern that had been gnawing at her.

"Ian, can we talk about the ethical lines of what we're planning to do?" Sarah started, her tone serious as she sat down across from him.

Ian looked up, his eyes tired but attentive. "Of course, Sarah. What's on your mind?"

"It's about how far we're willing to go to expose Wolfe. Using his tactics against him, engaging in psychological games... Are we risking becoming like him? Using manipulation to fight manipulation?" Sarah's voice was laced with genuine worry.

Ian sighed, leaning back in his chair. "That's a tough one. It's something I've been wrestling with too. We need to tread carefully to ensure we don't cross the line ourselves."

Sarah nodded, leaning forward, her hands clasped tightly together. "Exactly. And during this debate, if we push too hard or manipulate the narrative too aggressively, aren't we compromising our own integrity? How do we balance this?"

"We stick to the facts," Ian replied after a moment's thought. "We use the evidence we've gathered, and we present it clearly and without embellishment. Our goal isn't just to win an argument; it's to bring the truth to light."

"But what if the truth isn't enough to sway public opinion or to get the reaction we hope for from Wolfe? What if he turns the tables on us?" Sarah's concern was palpable.

Ian paused, considering her words. "Then we adapt, but we do it within the boundaries of our principles. We can be assertive and even cunning without stooping to his level of deceit."

Sarah seemed reassured but still somewhat uneasy. "I hope you're right, Ian. I guess I'm just worried about the slippery slope we might be on."

"I understand, and I share your concerns," Ian admitted, his tone sincere. "But remember why we're doing this. Wolfe's actions have harmed people, disrupted lives. We have a duty to stop him, and we're going to do it the right way."

The conversation shifted as they began to outline the specifics of their approach for the debate. "Let's define clear boundaries for our arguments," Ian suggested. "We avoid personal attacks, stick to exposing his actions and their consequences."

Sarah agreed, beginning to feel more grounded in their strategy. "And let's keep each other in check. If one of us starts veering too close to the edge, we pull back. Accountability, right?"

"Right," Ian confirmed with a nod. "We'll hold each other accountable. We're in this together, and we'll come out of it with our integrity intact."

As they continued to discuss and refine their approach, the burden of the ethical dilemma began to lighten. They were reassured by the framework they were putting in place, a strategy that allowed them to confront Wolfe effectively while maintaining their moral compass.

The meeting ended with both detectives feeling more confident in their plan and in their ability to handle the psychological and ethical complexities of their confrontation with Wolfe.

As Sarah left the office, Ian stayed behind, looking out the window into the darkening evening. The challenges ahead were daunting, but he felt prepared to face them, bolstered by the strength of his partnership with Sarah and their shared commitment to justice.

This internal conflict had not weakened their resolve but had deepened their understanding of the stakes involved. It had reaffirmed their commitment to operate within the boundaries of law and ethics, reinforcing their determination to bring Wolfe to justice the right way.

In the late hours of a brisk autumn evening, Detective Ian Mercer received an unexpected encrypted email. The message was cryptic, containing only a quote from a classic philosophical text and coordinates leading to an old, abandoned warehouse on the outskirts of Willow's End. Intrigued and cautious, Ian and Detective Sarah Langley decided to investigate, suspecting that Adrian Wolfe might be orchestrating another elaborate test or possibly setting a trap.

"'He who fights with monsters should be careful lest he thereby become a monster. And if you gaze long enough into an abyss, the abyss will also gaze into you.' Nietzsche," Ian read aloud as they drove to the location. "It's a warning, or maybe it's a challenge."

Sarah, navigating the dark roads, replied, "Wolfe knows we're onto him. This could be his way of trying to intimidate us, or worse, lure us into something we're not prepared for."

They arrived at the warehouse, the building looming ominously against the night sky. The place was deserted, the only sounds the howling wind and their own footsteps crunching on gravel as they approached cautiously.

"Stay sharp," Ian whispered, his hand resting on his weapon. They entered through a creaky metal door, their flashlights cutting through the darkness inside.

The warehouse was vast and filled with shadows that danced around the edges of their light. As they moved deeper, Ian spotted something: a projector set up in the center of the room, aimed at a blank wall. He signaled to Sarah, and they approached it.

Sarah examined the machine, finding it ready to play. With a nod from Ian, she pressed the start button. The wall lit up with a video of Adrian Wolfe, seated comfortably in an armchair, looking directly into the camera with a calm, almost serene expression.

"Detectives Mercer and Langley," Wolfe's recorded voice echoed in the hollow space. "I commend you for following the breadcrumbs. I trust you are finding our little game of cat and mouse stimulating. Philosophy, ethics, the nature of power—these are not just academic topics for us, are they?"

Ian's grip tightened on his flashlight. "He's mocking us," he muttered.

Wolfe continued, "I propose a meeting, a final confrontation where we can discuss our differing philosophies. Or perhaps you can try to arrest me—if you have sufficient evidence, that is."

The video ended with another set of coordinates and a time. It was for the next day, at a public park known for its sprawling gardens and numerous hideaways.

Sarah turned off the projector, her face set in a determined line. "It's a challenge, but also an opportunity. We could catch him in the act, especially if he tries to manipulate us in public."

Ian nodded, already formulating a plan. "We'll need backup, discreetly positioned. And we need to be prepared for anything. He won't make this easy or straightforward."

They left the warehouse, the echo of Wolfe's words lingering in the air. As they drove back, their conversation revolved around potential strategies and contingencies. They knew Wolfe would be prepared, likely with his own philosophical justifications for his actions.

"We need to outthink him, stay one step ahead," Sarah said, her mind racing through various scenarios.

"And we will," Ian replied confidently. "We know what he's capable of, and we know our own strengths. Tomorrow, we end this."

As they reached the precinct to prepare for the next day's encounter, both detectives felt the weight of the impending confrontation. It was more than just a physical meeting; it was a clash of ideals, a battle of wits and wills. But they were ready, armed not just with their skills and knowledge but with a firm resolve to see justice done.

Their plan was set, their team briefed, and as they left the briefing room, the first light of dawn was breaking over the horizon, signaling the beginning of what promised to be a decisive day.

Chapter 8
Personal Stakes

As the day of the crucial confrontation with Adrian Wolfe approached, Detective Ian Mercer found himself pacing the floor of his office, the early morning light casting long shadows across the room. His thoughts were a tumultuous mix of strategy and concern—not just for the success of their operation but for the safety of all involved. The personal risks had escalated dramatically, a reality that hit home when he received a thinly veiled threat against his family late the previous night.

Sarah Langley entered the office, her expression serious, holding a sealed envelope—a similar threat had been delivered to her home. "Ian, we need to consider the possibility that Wolfe is not just targeting us professionally but personally now."

Ian stopped pacing and took the envelope, placing it on his desk without opening it. "I know, Sarah. It's a whole new level of engagement. We're dealing with someone who doesn't hesitate to cross any

line to protect himself and his interests."

Sarah sighed, her concern evident. "We need to inform our families about the potential risks and make sure they're protected. I've already spoken to the department about security details for them."

Ian nodded, his jaw set. "I've done the same. It's one thing to put ourselves in the line of fire, quite another to expose our loved ones." The weight of leadership and responsibility was palpable in his voice.

The room was filled with a tense silence as both detectives processed the gravity of their situation. The personal stakes had never been higher, and the shadow of threat loomed over them, adding a stark urgency to their actions.

Ian finally broke the silence, turning his focus back to the operational aspects of their plan. "We need to tighten our security protocols, not just for our families but for everyone on the team. Wolfe's network is extensive, and we can't predict how far he'll go."

Sarah agreed, pulling up a digital map on the computer. "Let's go over the rendezvous point again. We need to ensure all possible escape routes are covered, and that our backup is ready to move in at a moment's notice."

As they meticulously reviewed every detail of their approach for the upcoming confrontation, Ian couldn't help but reflect on the broader implications of their battle with Wolfe. This was more than a mere law enforcement operation; it was a fight to protect the very fabric of their community and their personal lives from a man who sought to control and corrupt.

"We should also have a contingency plan in place if Wolfe escalates further," Ian suggested, his mind working through various scenarios.

"Agreed," said Sarah, her fingers flying over the keyboard as she annotated the map with additional notes and instructions. "And let's make sure our communications are secure. I don't want Wolfe or his people intercepting anything."

The rest of the day was spent in intense preparation and coordination with the rest of their team and other law enforcement agencies involved in the operation. By the end of it, Ian and Sarah felt as prepared as they could be, given the circumstances.

As the sun began to set, casting long shadows through the windows of Ian's office, he took a moment to stand quietly, looking out over the city he had sworn to protect. The risks were high, and the pressure was immense, but he knew that they were on the right side of this fight.

Sarah joined him at the window, her presence a steady reassurance. "We'll get through this, Ian. We'll bring him down and protect what's important."

Ian turned to her, a determined glint in his eyes. "Yes, we will. Let's do this."

As they left the precinct to head to the confrontation site, the weight of their shared resolve fortified them against the uncertainty of what was to come. They were not just fighting for justice; they were fighting for their community, their families, and each other.

In the secure confines of a nondescript surveillance van parked a discreet distance from the confrontation site, Detective Ian Mercer and Detective Sarah Langley were finalizing their strategy. However, the strain of the high stakes and the personal threats had begun to wear on them both, leading to an unusual friction between the typically cohesive partners.

Ian, looking over the surveillance feeds, spoke without turning. "We need to be absolutely certain Wolfe doesn't see any weakness in our approach today. Any hesitation on our part, and he'll exploit it."

Sarah, reviewing her notes, responded with a slight edge to her voice. "I'm well aware of that, Ian. But we also need to ensure we're not being reckless. Our families are at risk here. This isn't just about catching Wolfe anymore—it's about making sure we don't provoke him unnecessarily."

Ian turned sharply, his frustration apparent. "I'm not being reckless, Sarah. I'm trying to end this once and for all. The longer Wolfe is out there, the greater the danger to everyone."

"And I agree," Sarah retorted, her tone rising slightly. "But your push to confront Wolfe directly today might be exactly what he wants. He could be planning to use this situation to his advantage, to make us look aggressive or uncontrolled."

Ian sighed, running a hand through his hair. "Look, I know you're concerned, but we've planned this operation down to the last detail. We have backup, we have escape routes, and we have our team ready on every front. What more do you want?"

Sarah paused, her expression softening as she recognized the stress they were both under. "I want us to be smart, Ian. Not just tactical, but smart about how we're handling the bigger picture. Our families, remember? We can't just think like cops today; we have to think like parents, like spouses."

Ian's posture relaxed slightly as he acknowledged her point. "You're right. I know you're right. It's just hard to balance sometimes, especially with everything that's on the line."

The silence that followed was filled with the buzz of radio chatter and the soft hum of the van's equipment. After a moment, Sarah reached over to place a reassuring hand on Ian's arm. "We've always worked well together because we balance each other out. You push forward, and I make sure we don't fall over the edge. Let's not lose that now, not when it matters most."

Ian nodded, managing a small smile. "Thanks, Sarah. I needed to hear that. Let's make sure we both come out of this not just successful, but safe."

"Agreed," Sarah replied, returning his smile with one of her own. "Now, let's go over the plan one more time, make sure we're absolutely clear on each other's roles. No surprises."

As they went through their strategy again, both detectives felt their familiar partnership reasserting itself. The tension that had risen between them ebbed away, replaced by the mutual respect and understanding that had always marked their relationship. They were more than just partners; they were a team in the truest sense, and that bond was their greatest strength.

As the time for the operation drew near, Ian and Sarah checked their equipment and prepared to step out of the van. They knew the challenges ahead would be daunting, but together, they were ready to face whatever came their way with the confidence that only comes from trust and shared resolve.

As the operation to confront Adrian Wolfe progressed, Detectives Ian Mercer and Sarah Langley found themselves in a critical moment of their investigation. They were back in the surveillance van post-confrontation, poring over the recordings and other data they had collected during their interaction with Wolfe. It was then that Sarah stumbled upon something unexpected in the audio—a hidden, revealing clue that could potentially shift the entire direction of their case.

"Listen to this, Ian," Sarah said, her tone urgent as she replayed a segment of the recording. "Right here, Wolfe mentions a name— 'Marshall.' He's referring to someone we haven't focused on. Could this be a key associate we missed?"

Ian leaned in, listening intently as Wolfe's voice came through the speakers. "We must ensure Marshall is ready to move forward with the next phase..." Wolfe's words were clear, and the mention of a 'next phase' piqued their interest.

"Who's Marshall?" Ian pondered aloud, his brow furrowed. "This could be the break we need. If he's involved in planning, he might be central to Wolfe's operations."

Sarah was already on her laptop, typing rapidly. "I'm running the name through our database and cross-referencing with any of Wolfe's known associates and contacts. Give me a second."

As the computer processed her queries, Ian paced the small space, his mind racing with possibilities. "We've been so focused on Wolfe, we might have overlooked his support network. This Marshall could be a linchpin, someone who knows enough to help us take Wolfe down completely."

The computer beeped, and Sarah scanned the results. "Got something here. There's a James Marshall listed, but he's been off our radar. Looks like he's a financial advisor—lots of dealings with high-profile clients, including Wolfe."

Ian stopped pacing and turned to Sarah. "A financial advisor? That could explain the 'next phase' comment. Maybe it's not just ideological control Wolfe's after, but financial maneuvers as well."

Sarah nodded, pulling up more information. "It looks like Marshall has been quietly moving large sums of money for Wolfe. These transactions... they're cleverly disguised, but now that we know what we're looking for, I can trace them."

"Good work, Sarah," Ian commended, his energy renewed by the breakthrough. "Let's dig into Marshall's financials, see where the money's coming from and more importantly, where it's going. It might tell us more about Wolfe's plans."

Sarah's fingers flew over the keyboard as she navigated through financial records and transactions. "Here's something interesting—Marshall recently acquired a substantial share in several local businesses. The same ones Wolfe had been influencing."

Ian connected the dots aloud, "So Wolfe uses Marshall to solidify his financial hold over the community, under the guise of legitimate business deals. It's smart, it's covert, and it's incredibly dangerous."

As they uncovered more details, the scope of Wolfe's influence became even more alarming. Every piece of information added to their understanding of the complex web Wolfe had woven throughout Willow's End.

"We need to bring this to the DA," Ian decided, grabbing his phone to call their contact. "With Marshall's financial records as evidence, we can get warrants, maybe even bring him in for questioning."

Sarah was already compiling the data into a report. "I'll have everything ready. This could be the leverage we need to not only expose Wolfe but to start dismantling his entire operation."

The detectives worked late into the night, fortified by the significance of their discovery. The revelation about Marshall not only added a new dimension to their case but also provided a crucial pathway to understanding and disrupting Adrian Wolfe's broader plans.

As they finally stepped out of the van, stretching tired muscles and blinking against the bright lights of the precinct, Ian and Sarah felt a renewed sense of purpose. This was more than just a case to them—it was a fight for their community, and with each new clue, they were closer to winning it.

The night was deep and the air crisp as Detectives Ian Mercer and Sarah Langley approached the dimly lit warehouse where they believed Adrian Wolfe was orchestrating his most critical moves. The tip had come anonymously, but given the specifics it contained—right down to the time and security details—it was too precise to ignore. They approached cautiously, aware that Wolfe was becoming increasingly desperate and might not shy away from a direct confrontation.

The warehouse was secluded, nestled between derelict structures that had long ago been abandoned. As Ian and Sarah approached, the only sounds were their quiet footsteps and the distant hum of the city. They communicated through hand signals, their years of partnership allowing them to operate seamlessly in silence.

Ian checked his watch, the glow illuminating his focused expression. It was nearly midnight—the time the informant claimed Wolfe would be meeting with his closest associates. The detectives took positions at either side of the large metal door, Ian giving Sarah a nod before he slowly and silently eased the door open just enough to peer inside.

The interior was vast and shadowy, with high ceilings and rows of shelving units creating a labyrinthine environment. Sparse light filtered in through grimy skylights, casting long shadows. Ian's eyes adjusted to the darkness, scanning for any sign of movement.

Sarah gestured towards the back of the warehouse, where faint voices could be heard. The detectives moved stealthily in that direction, taking cover behind crates and keeping their presence undetected. As they drew closer, the voices became clearer, the tone urgent.

Ian paused, signaling Sarah to stay back as he edged closer to eavesdrop on the conversation. He could make out Wolfe's distinct voice, his tone both commanding and agitated. Wolfe was speaking about a plan that needed to be accelerated, his words laced with frustration over unexpected setbacks—setbacks that Ian and Sarah knew were the results of their own interventions.

After gathering enough audio evidence with the recorder hidden in his jacket, Ian gestured to Sarah that it was time to retreat. They had what they needed to escalate their case against Wolfe, and prolonging their presence in the warehouse posed unnecessary risk.

Retracing their steps, they moved back towards the entrance with careful precision, avoiding any loose debris that could betray their movements. Their exit was as silent as their entry, the door closing softly behind them.

Once outside, Ian and Sarah allowed themselves a moment to breathe. "We got him," Ian whispered, a mix of relief and resolve in his voice. "Once we get this recording to the DA, Wolfe's operations will start to unravel."

Sarah nodded, her eyes scanning the perimeter one last time before they headed back to their vehicle. "Tonight was a success, but we need to stay on our guard. Wolfe won't take this lightly."

As they drove away from the warehouse, the weight of their late-night venture began to lift. They had successfully infiltrated Wolfe's meeting, obtaining crucial evidence without detection. However, the night's success was tempered by the knowledge that Wolfe would be more cautious from now on, possibly even more dangerous.

Back at the precinct, Ian and Sarah filed their report and secured the recordings. The evidence was compelling, pointing not only to financial malfeasance but to deeper layers of corruption that tied Wolfe to several high-profile figures in the city.

As dawn approached, Ian looked out over the city from the precinct window, his thoughts on the challenges ahead. They were closer than ever to taking Wolfe down, but the path forward was fraught with danger, not just to their case but to their very lives. Yet, as the city slowly lightened with the rising sun, so too did Ian's resolve to see justice done, no matter the personal stakes.

Chapter 9
Breaking Point

The morning had started like any other in the Willow's End Police Department, but the normalcy was shattered when Detective Ian Mercer received a frantic call that turned the case against Adrian Wolfe into a personal nightmare. His voice strained, Ian listened as his wife explained in trembling tones that their daughter had not returned from her friend's house the previous night.

As Ian hung up the phone, his hands were shaking. Sarah noticed his distress immediately. "Ian, what's wrong?"

"It's Emily, my daughter. She's... she's been kidnapped," Ian managed to say, his voice breaking with emotion.

Sarah's expression shifted to one of shock and concern. "Oh my God, Ian, what can I do to help?"

"We need to move, now," Ian said, regaining his composure out of necessity. "We need to treat this like any other case to find her. Can you call the team? We need everyone on this."

Within minutes, the precinct was buzzing with heightened activity as officers and detectives mobilized. Ian led a briefing, outlining what little they knew. "We suspect this is Wolfe's doing. It's a move to get back at me, to derail our investigation."

Sarah added, organizing search teams and resources, "We'll start with tracking her last known locations. I'll also check for any demands or communications from the kidnapper."

The team quickly gathered surveillance footage from the area near Emily's last known location and began combing through it. Meanwhile,

Sarah worked to trace any calls or messages that might have been sent from Emily's phone.

After what felt like an agonizing stretch of time, an officer called out from his desk, "Detectives, you need to see this." He had found footage showing Emily being coerced into a black van by two unidentified individuals.

Ian rushed over, his eyes fixed on the screen. "Can we get a plate number? Any distinctive features on the van?"

The team worked to enhance the image, but the plate was obscured by mud. However, one of the detectives noticed a sticker on the back window. "Look here, this might be something. It's a logo—looks like a wolf."

"A wolf..." Ian's voice trailed off as he made the connection. "Wolfe's symbol. He's sending a message."

Sarah, who had been coordinating with the tech team, turned to Ian. "We've got a partial hit on the van from a traffic camera two blocks from where Emily was taken. It's not much, but it's a start."

"Alright, let's get units out looking for that van. Broadcast the description to all patrols. I want roadblocks set up at all major exits from the city," Ian ordered, his tone authoritative yet strained.

As the team dispersed to carry out their tasks, Ian took a moment to gather himself. Sarah approached, her concern evident. "Ian, maybe you should—"

"No," Ian interrupted, his resolve clear despite his evident worry. "I'm not stepping back. Wolfe did this to get to me, and I'm not giving him the satisfaction of seeing me break."

Sarah nodded, understanding his need to stay involved. "Okay, Ian. But remember, we're here for you. You're not alone in this."

The crisis had escalated the stakes to their highest point, transforming a professional battle into a deeply personal one. As Ian coordinated the search for his daughter, his heart ached with fear and anger, but he remained focused. He knew that giving in to despair would not help Emily; only his skills as a detective could bring her back safely.

The hours passed with teams scouring the city, following up on every lead, no matter how small. Ian stayed at the heart of the operation, driven by a father's need to protect his child, and by a detective's determination to bring the perpetrators to justice. The situation was critical, but Ian and his team were resolute. They would find Emily and bring her home, no matter what it took.

Hours turned into a full night as the search for Emily Mercer intensified, yet each passing moment seemed only to deepen Detective Ian Mercer's sense of desperation and isolation. Inside the cramped confines of the police department's command center, Ian and Detective Sarah Langley pored over maps and incoming data, their faces etched with fatigue and stress.

"Ian, we've expanded the search perimeter, and I've got two more units assigned to monitor all known associates of Wolfe," Sarah reported, trying to inject a note of hope into her voice.

Ian, who hadn't moved from in front of the monitors for hours, rubbed his eyes wearily. "Thank you, Sarah. What about the traffic cams and public transport footage? Anything there?"

"We're still combing through it. The resolution on some of the older cameras isn't great, but we're enhancing what we can," Sarah responded, scrolling through a digital file list.

Ian sighed deeply, the weight of his daughter's abduction visibly bearing down on him. "I keep thinking about the last thing I said to her. It was just a normal goodbye. If I'd known..."

Sarah placed a reassuring hand on his shoulder. "You couldn't have known, Ian. This isn't on you. We're going to find her."

Just then, their conversation was interrupted by a junior detective rushing over with a phone in hand. "Detective Mercer, we have a call. The caller ID was masked, but they asked specifically for you."

Ian's heart skipped as he took the phone. "This is Mercer."

The distorted voice on the other end was chillingly calm. "Detective Mercer, your persistence is admirable, but it's time to reconsider your actions. You're causing more trouble than you realize."

Ian's voice was steady, despite the turmoil inside. "What do you want?"

"It's simple. Back off from the Wolfe case. Stop your investigation, or you won't like the consequences," the voice threatened, the implication clear.

Ian tightened his grip on the phone. "If you harm my daughter—"

The caller cut him off. "The choice is yours, Detective. Remember, not all battles are worth the casualties they cause."

The line went dead. Ian stood frozen for a moment, the phone still pressed to his ear. Sarah watched him, her expression a mix of anger and concern. "Ian, we're not backing down. We're going to get Emily back and nail Wolfe, no matter what his thugs say."

Ian finally set the phone down, his resolve hardening. "You're right, Sarah. We're not giving in to his threats. But how do we protect Emily and continue the case? Wolfe isn't playing by any rules we know."

Sarah leaned in, lowering her voice. "We work smarter. We keep pressure on Wolfe's network, but we also tighten our security around what matters most. Your family, the team—everyone. We make Wolfe believe he can push us, but without giving him actual leverage."

Ian considered her words, a plan slowly forming in his mind. "We need a decoy operation. Something to make Wolfe think he's steering the game, while we close in from another angle."

"Exactly. And I think I know just the approach. Let's set up a fake pullback from the investigation. Make it look like we're scaling down due to 'resource constraints'. Meanwhile, we'll use all available undercover assets to track down Emily," Sarah suggested, her mind working through the logistics.

Ian nodded, feeling a slight lift in the oppressive weight he'd been carrying. "Let's do it. Set up the decoy, and I'll coordinate with the undercover teams. We're not just going to find Emily; we're going to end this with Wolfe behind bars."

As they set their plan into motion, the command center that had felt like a cage began to feel more like a war room. Each step was calculated, each decision weighed with precision. The sense of desperation that had threatened to overwhelm Ian transformed into a sharp focus on the tasks ahead. The stakes had never been higher, but so too was their determination to fight not just for justice, but for family, for Emily.

The tension was palpable in the cramped quarters of the surveillance van as Detectives Ian Mercer and Sarah Langley, along with a team of forensic experts, examined the latest batch of evidence collected near the outskirts of the city. The break in the case came unexpectedly when a local hiker found a piece of torn fabric caught on a fence near an old forest trail known to be a lesser-used route out of town.

"Could this be from Emily's clothing?" Ian asked, holding up the fabric under a bright light, his voice tight with controlled urgency.

Sarah, who had been coordinating with the search teams via radio, glanced over. "It's possible. It matches the description of what she was wearing when she was last seen. I'll send a photo to her mother just to confirm."

As they waited for confirmation, the forensic team worked to gather any traces of DNA or other forensic evidence from the fabric. Minutes later, Sarah's phone buzzed, and she read the incoming message. "It's confirmed, Ian. That's part of her jacket. She was definitely taken through here."

Ian's jaw clenched at the news, his eyes reflecting a mixture of relief and renewed determination. "Alright, this is good. This gives us a more focused search area. Let's get the dogs and additional units out here immediately."

Sarah was already on the radio, her words crisp and authoritative. "All units, we have a confirmed clue related to the Mercer kidnapping case. I need search teams and K-9 units redirected to the Old Forest trailhead. Let's move quickly and quietly. Time is of the essence."

As the teams mobilized, Ian and Sarah decided to follow the trail themselves, guided by the search dogs. The forest was dense and the path unclear in places, but the urgency of finding Emily pushed them forward. Each snap of a twig underfoot sounded alarmingly loud in the quiet of the forest.

"Keep your eyes open for anything else she might have dropped," Ian reminded Sarah as they navigated through the underbrush. "Anything that might give us more clues about where they were heading."

Sarah nodded, her eyes scanning the ground and the surrounding area. "I'm on it. And Ian, remember, we're not just looking for Emily now. We need to find any sign of her captors too. There could be more than one."

As they progressed, the lead search dog suddenly became more agitated, its barking more frequent. The handler signaled to Ian and Sarah. "The dog's picked up a stronger scent. We're close to something."

Heart pounding with both hope and fear, Ian quickened his pace, Sarah right beside him. They emerged into a clearing where the remnants of a recently abandoned campsite lay. A cold fire pit, a discarded rope, and signs of a hasty departure suggested they had just missed capturing the captors.

"This is it. They were here," Ian said, examining the site. "Get CSU down here to process everything. Maybe they left behind something we can use."

As Sarah coordinated with the Crime Scene Unit, Ian stood at the edge of the clearing, his eyes searching the dense trees beyond. The realization that Emily had been so close weighed heavily on him.

"We'll find her, Ian," Sarah assured him, coming to stand beside him. "We're on the right path now. Let's keep moving."

The race against time became even more frantic as they pushed deeper into the forest, guided by the scent trail and determined to rescue Emily. Each moment was critical, and with the trail growing warmer, Ian and Sarah steeled themselves for what they might find, ready to face whatever was necessary to bring Emily home safely.

As the search intensified, the teams pushed further into the dense woodland, the urgency palpable in every step. Detective Ian Mercer and Detective Sarah Langley, leading a team of seasoned officers, advanced cautiously. The clues uncovered at the abandoned campsite had provided them with a fresh trail to follow, which now led to a dilapidated cabin hidden deep in the forest.

The cabin, obscured by overgrown brush and partly cloaked in shadows, appeared as a sinister silhouette against the fading light. Ian signaled for quiet and motioned for the team to spread out. The rustling of leaves underfoot seemed deafening in the tense silence that enveloped the area.

Sarah whispered into her radio, coordinating with the perimeter teams. "Positions are set. We're ready to move on your command."

Ian nodded, his expression set in grim determination. He addressed his team in a low, controlled voice. "Remember, our primary objective is Emily's safety. We go in quietly. No heroics. We do this by the book."

With a hand signal, the team approached the cabin. As they drew nearer, the faint sound of movement from inside confirmed their worst fears — they were not alone. Ian's heart pounded with a mix of fear and resolve; this was the moment they had prepared for.

The entry team, led by Ian and Sarah, positioned themselves at the front door. Ian counted down with his fingers, and on zero, the door was breached. The team moved in swiftly, their movements practiced and precise.

Inside, the cabin was dimly lit, the only light coming from a single, flickering bulb. The air was stale, and the smell of mold lingered. As the team cleared each room, the tension mounted — until they reached the back room.

There, tied to a chair, was Emily. Her eyes, wide with fear, filled with tears as she saw her father. Ian's heart broke at the sight, but he maintained his composure for her sake. "It's okay, Emily. You're safe now," he assured her as he quickly moved to untie her.

Sarah kept her weapon trained on the room's two exits, while other officers secured the area. "Perimeter teams, suspect still at large. Keep your eyes open," she communicated through her radio.

With Emily freed, Ian gently wrapped his jacket around her shoulders, his relief palpable but his senses still on high alert. The cabin was now secure, but the kidnapper had evaded capture, leaving them with more questions than answers.

As they escorted Emily out of the cabin, the forest around them seemed to exhale, the tension dissipating slightly with each step towards safety. Back at the rendezvous point, paramedics immediately attended to Emily, ensuring she was unharmed physically, though the emotional scars were evident.

Ian stayed by her side, his relief at her safety tempered by the knowledge that Wolfe, or someone from his network, was still out there. "We're going to find who did this," Ian promised Emily quietly, a promise he extended to himself and his team.

Sarah, watching Ian with Emily, felt a profound respect for her partner's strength and dedication. She turned to the officers, her voice firm. "Let's wrap up here. We need to process the scene, gather any evidence we can. This isn't over."

The operation had been a success, but the night's events had changed them all. The personal stakes of their mission had never been clearer, nor more deeply felt. As they prepared to leave the forest, the weight of continuing their fight against Wolfe hung over them, a somber reminder of the dangers they still faced.

The drive back to the precinct was quiet, each member of the team lost in their thoughts, the cabin's shadow lingering like a specter. But within that silence was a resolve, hardened by the night's trials — they would see this through, no matter what lay ahead.

Chapter 10
Mid-Novel Climax

The quiet of the early morning hours at Willow's End Police Department was a stark contrast to the adrenaline-fueled chaos that had engulfed the place just hours before. Detective Ian Mercer and Detective Sarah Langley, both physically and emotionally drained, sat in Ian's office, a silent understanding between them that their recent ordeal had changed them in ways they were only beginning to comprehend.

Ian broke the silence, his voice weary but relieved. "I can't thank you enough, Sarah. If it weren't for you and the team, I don't know what would have happened to Emily."

Sarah, who had been staring blankly at a stack of reports on her desk, looked up and managed a small smile. "It's what we do, Ian. We look out for each other. But how is Emily? Really?"

Ian leaned back in his chair, the lines of fatigue evident on his face. "She's shaken, obviously. We're going to start seeing a counselor next week. It's... it's going to be a long road for her, for all of us."

Sarah nodded sympathetically. "And how are you holding up? Being a detective and a dad, handling a case this personal... I can't even imagine."

Ian sighed, running a hand through his hair. "I'm not sure yet. It feels like I've been running on autopilot. Now that she's safe, it's all starting to hit me. The fear, the anger... I'm just trying to process it all."

The room fell silent again, each detective lost in their own thoughts until Sarah spoke up, shifting the conversation towards their ongoing mission. "We can't let up on Wolfe. This attack... it was a message. He's trying to intimidate us, throw us off balance."

Ian's jaw clenched at the mention of Wolfe. "He's escalated things to a level I didn't think he'd go. But you're right, we can't back down. We need to strike back, hard. We need to dismantle his network before he regroups."

Sarah leaned forward, her expression determined. "We've got a lot of evidence from the cabin, and the leads from the campsite might still pay off. We're close, Ian. We can do this."

Ian nodded, his resolve hardening. "We'll review everything we have. Every transaction, every communication. We'll find his weaknesses and we'll expose him. For Emily, for the community."

Sarah's eyes met Ian's, a fire kindling in them. "Let's put a plan together. We can use the public sympathy from Emily's case to leverage more resources, maybe even get the FBI more involved."

Ian considered this, the gears turning. "Good idea. I'll reach out to my contact there. We'll need all the help we can get."

As they delved into planning their next moves, the room was filled with a renewed sense of purpose. The personal stakes had never been clearer, nor more motivating. With each strategy discussed and each resource allocated, Ian and Sarah not only reinforced their professional bond but also their personal commitment to justice.

"We're not just doing our jobs," Ian stated, a new strength in his voice. "We're fighting back against someone who thinks he can control and destroy lives. We're showing him that he's wrong."

Sarah stood, gathering her things. "Let's get to it then. The sooner we take Wolfe down, the sooner we can all breathe a little easier."

As Sarah left the office, Ian took a moment to look at a photo of Emily on his desk, her smile a bittersweet reminder of what they were fighting for. With a deep breath, he stood up, his fatigue pushed aside by determination. The fight was far from over, and Ian Mercer was ready to lead the charge.

In the solitude of his home, Detective Ian Mercer sat at his dining room table, surrounded by case files and notes that seemed to spread out like a map of the complex journey he had traveled. The quiet of the night was a stark contrast to the turmoil within him, reflecting a palpable tension between his professional duties and personal trials. It was here, amid the silent whispers of his family home, that Ian found himself grappling with the magnitude of his commitment to bringing Adrian Wolfe to justice.

The phone rang, slicing through the stillness. It was Sarah Langley, her voice carrying a mix of urgency and concern. "Ian, we've had a breakthrough with the financial leads. We've found connections between Wolfe and several offshore accounts. This could be what we need to tie him directly to the illegal activities."

Ian's response was measured, his fatigue evident. "That's great, Sarah. Let's meet first thing in the morning to plan our next steps."

"You sound tired, Ian. Make sure you're not pushing yourself too hard," Sarah advised, her tone softening.

"I'm fine," Ian replied, though his voice betrayed the strain he felt. "I just... I've been thinking about what all this means. The risks we're taking, what I'm asking of everyone involved."

Sarah understood the depth of Ian's reflection. "It's a lot, but remember, you're not doing this alone. We're all in this together because we believe in what we're doing. We believe in you."

Ian paused, considering her words. "Thanks, Sarah. I guess I just needed to hear that tonight."

After hanging up, Ian sat back, his eyes drifting to a framed photograph of his daughter Emily, taken before the kidnapping. The image of her smiling face was a stark reminder of the personal cost of this battle. It was this moment, under the quiet gaze of his daughter's captured joy, that Ian's resolve crystallized.

He spoke aloud to himself, a declaration in the solitude of his home. "This ends now. Wolfe's reign of fear ends now. I will not let this man control any more lives, threaten any more families."

The next morning, Ian arrived at the precinct with a renewed sense of purpose. He walked with determined strides into the briefing room where Sarah and the rest of the team were assembling.

"I want to thank you all," Ian began, addressing his team with a newfound vigor. "Last night, I was reminded of why we do what we do. It's not just about upholding the law. It's about protecting the innocent, about standing up to those who would manipulate and coerce to serve their own ends."

Sarah watched Ian, seeing the shift in his demeanor. "What's the plan, Ian?"

"We're going to use every piece of evidence, every resource at our disposal to bring Wolfe in. No stone unturned," Ian declared. "Sarah, let's get the warrants ready. I want raids on every property linked to those offshore accounts by tonight."

The team mobilized quickly, energized by Ian's leadership and the imminent prospect of action. As they dispersed to carry out their assignments, Sarah approached Ian.

"You really meant what you said, didn't you?" she asked.

Ian nodded, his gaze firm. "More than ever. We're going to show Wolfe that he picked the wrong town, the wrong families to mess with. We're going to show him that justice isn't just an ideal—it's a reality, and it's coming for him."

As Ian and Sarah left the briefing room to prepare for the day's critical operations, there was a palpable sense of unity and resolve. This was more than a turning point in the case—it was a turning point in Ian's personal journey, a reaffirmation of his commitment not just as a detective, but as a protector of his community.

The atmosphere in the strategy room was electric as Detective Ian Mercer led a tactical meeting with his team. Maps and digital screens lit up the room, displaying various points of interest related to Adrian Wolfe's operations. As Ian pointed to each location, he delineated the roles and responsibilities for each team member, ensuring that everyone understood the plan and the part they played.

"This operation is about precision," Ian stated, his voice commanding the room's attention. "Each team has a specific target. We've coordinated with federal agencies to ensure backup is available if needed. I want clean entries, minimal confrontation, and a focus on securing evidence."

Sarah Langley, overseeing logistics, distributed the final copies of the operational plan to each team leader. "Check your gear before you depart. Communications need to be clear and constant. We can't afford any breakdowns in the field."

As the team leaders left to prepare their units, Ian pulled Sarah aside to discuss the broader implications of their plan. "Once we strike, Wolfe will know we're closing in. He might try to go underground, or worse, retaliate. We need to be prepared for all scenarios."

Sarah nodded, her expression serious. "I've arranged for surveillance on all known associates. If Wolfe moves, we'll know about it. And the protection details for our families are doubled. We're locked down tight."

Ian looked over the room, where the remaining members of the team were checking their equipment and reviewing their assignments. He felt a surge of pride and responsibility for the group he was about to lead into a potentially volatile situation.

"We're doing more than just taking down a criminal," Ian addressed those present. "We're sending a message that our town, our community, isn't a place where corruption and manipulation can thrive. What we do today will resonate beyond just this case. It's about setting a precedent."

As preparations continued, Ian's focus shifted to ensuring that his team felt supported and understood the significance of their roles. He moved among the groups, offering words of encouragement and addressing any last-minute concerns.

"Remember, everyone comes home today," Ian reiterated, meeting the eyes of each team member. "We look out for each other out there. Stay sharp, stay safe."

The commitment in the room was palpable, with each member geared up and ready to move out. As the teams departed the precinct, the weight of the operation settled on Ian's shoulders—not just the tactical burden, but the emotional one. He knew that the outcomes of the day would affect more than just the legal standings of those involved; they would impact lives, families, and the very fabric of their community.

Back in his office, Ian took a moment to reflect. He glanced at a photograph of Emily, a reminder of why he fought so hard, why he pushed himself and his team to face such dangers. It wasn't just about law enforcement; it was about protecting and preserving the way of life that his community cherished.

As the clock ticked down to the operation's commencement, Ian reviewed the plan once more. Every detail had been accounted for, every contingency considered. He allowed himself a brief moment of quiet, gathering his resolve.

Today, he thought, we turn the tide. Today, we show that justice is more than an ideal—it's an action, and it's upheld by those brave enough to stand in its defense.

With a deep breath, Ian left his office to join his team, ready to lead them into one of the most significant days of their careers. The strategic planning and team strengthening had culminated in this moment, a testament to their dedication and unity in the face of adversity.

The operation had commenced with clinical precision. Teams moved into their designated locations, each unit synchronizing their actions with the others. Detective Ian Mercer and Detective Sarah Langley led one of the primary raid teams, focused on a warehouse on the outskirts of town that intelligence had pinpointed as a critical node in Adrian Wolfe's network.

As they breached the warehouse door, the team was met with the dim, echoing vastness of an apparently abandoned building. Rows of crates and boxes lined the space, each shadow potentially concealing a threat. Methodically, the team cleared each section, their movements practiced and silent, save for the soft commands issued under breath.

Ian, leading from the front, signaled for two officers to check a suspicious, partially enclosed area in the back. As they approached, the sound of something shifting inside caused a momentary halt. With a swift motion, the officers flung the enclosure open, revealing not the stash of incriminating evidence they had hoped for, but a sophisticated set-up of electronic equipment and monitors—seemingly abandoned in haste.

The discovery was significant, but not in the way Ian had anticipated. As the tech specialists swept in to analyze the equipment, it became apparent that the operation had been compromised. The monitors displayed live feeds from various locations around the city, including several they had planned to raid that day.

"It looks like Wolfe was warned. He's been monitoring law enforcement movements," one of the techs reported, his voice tense with frustration.

Ian's jaw tightened as he processed the implications. "Can we trace any of the feeds? Find out where they're being controlled from?" he asked, hoping for some way to salvage the operation.

"We'll need some time, but it's possible," the tech replied, already beginning to interface with the equipment.

Sarah joined Ian, her expression grim. "This explains the lack of resistance. He knew we were coming."

Ian nodded, frustration evident in his voice. "We've got to assume all our targets today have been compromised. We need to pull back and reassess."

The setback was a heavy blow to the morale of the team. As they withdrew from the warehouse, Ian radioed the other units, instructing them to abort their missions and regroup. The ride back to the precinct was quiet, each officer lost in their thoughts, contemplating the unexpected turn of events.

Back at the precinct, Ian convened an impromptu debrief in the strategy room. The atmosphere was tense, the room filled with a palpable sense of urgency and disappointment. As he looked around at the faces of his team, Ian knew he had to address the setback head-on.

"We've hit a snag, but this isn't the end. It's a setback, nothing more," Ian began, his voice steady despite the turmoil. "Wolfe is clever, but he's not invincible. He's shown his hand, and now we know just how much he's invested in keeping his operations hidden."

Sarah stepped in, her tone supportive. "We also know he's scared. He wouldn't have gone to these lengths if he wasn't feeling threatened. We're close, and he knows it."

The team listened, their earlier defeat turning slowly into a renewed determination. Ian continued, outlining the next steps. "We're going to plug the leaks in our operation. We tighten security, reevaluate our intel, and most importantly, we keep pressing. Wolfe is running out of places to hide."

As the meeting adjourned, the team dispersed to begin the hard work of rebuilding and restructuring their approach. The unexpected discovery at the warehouse had been a significant setback, but it had also provided them with valuable insight into Wolfe's operations and his desperation.

Ian and Sarah stayed behind, reviewing the warehouse's surveillance footage once more, looking for any detail they might have missed. Their resolve had been tested, but their commitment to bringing Wolfe to justice was unshaken. This fight was personal, and they were not about to back down, no matter what surprises lay in store.

Chapter 11
New Alliances

In the wake of their latest operational setback, Detectives Ian Mercer and Sarah Langley realized that to effectively dismantle Adrian Wolfe's far-reaching network, they would need to extend their circle of trust and resources. They arranged meetings with various potential allies, ranging from local law enforcement branches to federal agencies, hoping to fortify their efforts with additional expertise and manpower.

The chapter opens with Ian and Sarah preparing the conference room for the arrival of federal agents. They meticulously arranged chairs around the large table, which was laden with files and evidence photos, each item a testament to their thorough investigation.

"Ian, do you think they'll be on board with our approach?" Sarah asked, her voice tinged with a mix of hope and anxiety.

"We have to make them see the bigger picture, Sarah. It's not just about taking down one man; it's about rooting out an entire network that's poisoned this town," Ian responded, straightening a stack of files.

As the federal agents filed in, Ian started the presentation, his tone firm yet inviting. "Thank you for coming. We're here today because we've uncovered a web of manipulation and crime that extends beyond anything we've anticipated. We need your help to bring this to an end."

One of the agents, a stern-looking woman named Agent Ramirez, looked over the evidence laid out before her. "You've done impressive work, Detective Mercer. But what exactly are you asking from us?"

Ian exchanged a glance with Sarah before replying, "We're asking for manpower, surveillance resources, and forensic support. We believe Wolfe's operations are not just a local threat but potentially have national implications."

Sarah chimed in, reinforcing Ian's points with precise details about their needs, "We also require legal expertise to navigate the charges we intend to bring against Wolfe and his associates. This isn't just a murder investigation; it involves complex financial crimes and psychological manipulation."

The agents conferred among themselves, whispering and nodding as they reviewed the documents provided. After a moment, Agent Ramirez spoke, "Your investigation has certainly uncovered a significant threat. We can provide the resources you're asking for. However, we'll need complete transparency and cooperation from your team."

Ian nodded, a slight smile breaking through his usually stoic demeanor. "You'll have it. We want nothing more than to see justice served."

As the meeting adjourned, Sarah and Ian stayed back to discuss the new alliance with the federal team. "This could really change the game," Sarah remarked, gathering the papers.

Ian, who was usually reserved about showing optimism, allowed himself a moment to feel hopeful. "Yes, it could. Let's make sure we use this opportunity to its fullest."

The chapter concludes with Ian and Sarah organizing the influx of new resources and personnel into their operation. As they left the precinct together, the weight of their responsibility was matched only by their renewed determination to end Wolfe's reign of terror. The partnership with the federal agents not only brought new allies into the fold but also strengthened the bond between Ian and Sarah, setting the stage for the intensified efforts to come.

The strategic alliances formed with federal agencies brought an unexpected asset to Detective Ian Mercer and Detective Sarah Langley's team—a former insider of the secretive club, Evelyn Sharp. Evelyn, having survived one of the club's orchestrated ordeals, offered a unique perspective and invaluable insights into the workings and members of the club.

In a small, secure room within the precinct, Ian and Sarah met with Evelyn for the first time. The air was tense, as trust was a commodity hard earned in their line of work.

"Ms. Sharp, thank you for agreeing to meet with us," Ian began, extending a hand cautiously.

Evelyn, a woman in her mid-thirties with sharp features and a cautious demeanor, accepted his handshake. "Detective Mercer, Detective Langley, I'm here because I believe you can stop them—stop Wolfe," she said, her voice firm despite the underlying strain.

Sarah invited Evelyn to take a seat. "We've gathered quite a bit of information about the club's activities, but your insider perspective could be the key to dismantling them completely. Can you tell us how you became involved with them?"

Evelyn nodded, taking a deep breath before speaking. "I was recruited by Wolfe himself. I am—or was—a psychologist. Wolfe admired my thesis on behavioral manipulation. At first, it was all academic discussions, but then I was invited to the club meetings. That's when I saw the true nature of what was happening."

Ian leaned forward, his interest piqued. "What exactly did you witness at these meetings?"

"They weren't just discussions. They were planning sessions for... experiments, on unsuspecting people. The aim was to manipulate their choices, control them without them knowing. I objected once I realized, and that's when I became a target," Evelyn recounted, her eyes darkening with the memory.

Sarah took notes, then asked, "How did you manage to get out?"

"It wasn't easy. I had to fake complete loyalty while gathering evidence. When I had enough, I escaped and went to the authorities, but Wolfe has people everywhere... That's why I'm here now. I want to help bring him down," Evelyn explained.

Ian exchanged a glance with Sarah, sensing the opportunity and the risks involved. "Your information could significantly advance our case. Do you have documents or anything that could directly link Wolfe and the club to these activities?"

"Yes, I took files, recordings. It's all hidden, for safety. I can take you to them, but we need to be careful. Wolfe... he's dangerous, and he's watching," Evelyn warned.

Sarah nodded, understanding the stakes. "We'll take every precaution. Your safety is our priority. Can you map out the club's hierarchy for us? Understanding their structure will help us know who we are dealing with."

Evelyn agreed and began outlining the key figures and their roles within the club. As she spoke, Ian visualized the network, recognizing some names from their own investigations.

"This is incredibly helpful, Evelyn. With your testimony and the evidence you've gathered, we can make a strong case against Wolfe and his associates," Ian said, feeling a renewed sense of hope.

The meeting continued with discussions on the logistics of retrieving the hidden evidence and planning for potential fallout. Evelyn's cooperation marked a significant turning point in the investigation, providing Ian and Sarah not just with crucial information but with a tangible link to the inner workings of their adversaries.

As Evelyn left the room, escorted by an officer to ensure her safety, Ian and Sarah remained behind, digesting the new information. "This changes everything, Sarah. It's bigger than we thought, but now we've got something solid to strike with," Ian remarked, his resolve hardening.

Sarah looked at Ian, sensing the weight of their responsibility. "We're going to bring him down, Ian. With Evelyn's help, Wolfe's days are numbered."

The chapter closed with a sense of cautious optimism. The alliance with Evelyn Sharp brought new allies into the fold, deepening the investigation and solidifying the team's resolve to end the reign of terror orchestrated by Adrian Wolfe and his secretive club.

With Evelyn Sharp's insights illuminating the inner workings of the secretive club, Detectives Ian Mercer and Sarah Langley were poised to orchestrate a coordinated strike against multiple targets simultaneously. The planning required meticulous attention to detail and coordination with both local and federal forces, ensuring that the operation would cripple Adrian Wolfe's network in one decisive blow.

In the newly established operations center, filled with maps and digital displays, Ian and Sarah, along with federal agents and tactical commanders, huddled over a large table strewn with layouts of the targeted locations.

"We have to be precise and synchronized. Timing here is critical; we hit them all before Wolfe can warn his associates," Ian stated, pointing to the map highlighting the strategic points of interest.

Agent Ramirez, overseeing the federal involvement, reviewed the plan. "Each team has been briefed. We'll have eyes on all exits, and communications will be jammed at the moment of entry to prevent any last-minute alerts between locations."

Sarah, focused on logistics, added, "Evelyn provided the layout of Wolfe's main hideout. There are underground escape routes we need to cover. I suggest we deploy surveillance drones to monitor those exits."

The room buzzed with the low murmur of officers and agents coordinating roles. Tactical team leaders approached the table, confirming their parts in the operation.

"Teams Alpha and Bravo will take the north and south entrances. Team Charlie, you're on aerial support. Remember, non-lethal force whenever possible—we need them alive and talking," directed one of the tactical commanders.

Ian, his expression somber, acknowledged the stakes. "This is about more than arrests. We're dismantling a network that's terrorized this community. Let's bring them in and end this."

As the meeting progressed, Sarah took a moment to discuss the legal groundwork with the prosecutors who had joined the preparation. "We need to ensure that the evidence collected during the raids is admissible in court. Let's double-check the warrants and the specific legal language we're using."

One of the prosecutors, a seasoned litigator named Helen, reassured her, "We've reviewed all the documentation. Everything's in order. Once you bring them in, we'll handle it from there."

In the corner of the room, Ian pulled up surveillance footage on a laptop, analyzing the behaviors and patterns observed at one of the club's frequented spots. His focus was broken by a quiet conversation between two analysts discussing the potential for cyber interference from Wolfe's tech-savvy allies.

"We've set up countermeasures for any cyber-attacks. They won't be able to delete or encrypt their data before we have access," one analyst explained.

With the strategic elements in place, the room shifted from planning to readiness, the tension palpable but focused. Ian gathered his thoughts, then addressed the room with a finality that underscored the importance of their task.

"Everyone, let's keep in mind why we're here. We've got a chance to right some serious wrongs. Stay sharp, watch your partner's back, and let's clean up our town."

As the teams dispersed to finalize preparations, Ian and Sarah shared a brief moment of quiet solidarity. "We've come a long way, Sarah. Thanks for standing by," Ian said, his tone appreciative.

Sarah nodded, her resolve clear. "We finish this together, Ian. Let's see it through."

The chapter concluded with the strike teams moving out, their vehicles quietly leaving the precinct under the cover of darkness. Each team member was acutely aware of the part they played in this intricate dance of justice. The night ahead would be long and fraught with peril, but the resolve to dismantle Wolfe's empire had never been stronger.

As the night wore on and the hour to initiate the strike drew near, the weight of their imminent task settled heavily on Detective Ian Mercer. He found himself in his office, the maps and photos of their targets spread out before him, each a small battlefield in its own right. The quiet of the room contrasted sharply with the storm of thoughts raging in his mind.

Sarah Langley, noticing Ian's prolonged silence and stillness, stepped into his office, her expression one of concern mixed with resolve. "Ian, everything's ready. Teams are in position waiting for our go. You okay to do this?"

Ian looked up, his eyes betraying a flicker of doubt. "I know we've planned everything down to the second, Sarah, but what if we're missing something? What if Wolfe has anticipated this move too?"

Sarah approached the desk, her voice steady. "Ian, we've covered every angle. Evelyn's information gave us the edge we needed. Wolfe won't see us coming, not this time."

Ian nodded slowly, but his gaze returned to the maps. "It's not just about catching Wolfe or dismantling his network. It's about the people we might hurt inadvertently. The responsibility feels overwhelming."

Recognizing the burden Ian was shouldering, Sarah leaned against the desk, her tone softening. "I get it. The stakes are high, and so are the risks. But think about how many lives we're going to save if we pull this off. We're ending a cycle of manipulation and fear. You taught me that we do what we must, not because it's easy, but because it's right."

Ian let out a slow breath, the weight of his decisions as palpable as the silence around them. "You're right, Sarah. It's just... every time I think about what could go wrong—"

Sarah cut him off, her voice firm yet reassuring. "And every time you think that, remember how many things have already gone right because of your decisions. You have a gift, Ian. Not just your... ability, but your instinct, your drive to seek justice. That's why I followed you into this, why the team believes in this mission."

A small smile tugged at the corner of Ian's mouth, her words grounding him more than he expected. "Thanks, Sarah. I needed to hear that."

"Just speaking the truth," Sarah said, pushing off from the desk to stand upright. "Now, let's go and show Wolfe that he picked the wrong town and the wrong people to mess with."

Ian stood up, feeling a renewed sense of purpose, bolstered by Sarah's unwavering support and the collective resolve of their team. "You're right. It's time to end this."

Together, they left the office, heading towards the operations room where the rest of the team awaited their final orders. The corridors of the precinct felt different tonight—charged with a collective anticipation and readiness for the task ahead.

As they entered the operations room, the eyes of their team members met theirs, each pair reflecting a mix of nerves and determination. Ian stepped forward, addressing the room with a commander's presence. "This is it. We've prepared, we've planned, and now we act. Keep sharp, keep safe, and let's take them down."

Nods and murmurs of agreement filled the room, the team's spirits lifted by Ian's leadership and the imminent action. As the final checks were made and the last confirmations received, Ian and Sarah shared a brief, knowing glance. No words were needed—both knew the depth of the night's importance, not just for their careers but for the very soul of Willow's End.

The chapter closed as the teams moved out, the silence of the precinct giving way to the soft hum of vehicles disappearing into the night. The city lay ahead, unknowingly on the cusp of a pivotal change, with Ian Mercer and Sarah Langley leading the charge to reclaim their community from the shadows that had long plagued it.

Chapter 12
Unraveling the Web

The early hours of the morning found Willow's End under a blanket of darkness, its usual nighttime stillness disrupted by the quiet thrum of engines and the muted crackle of radios. In various locations, members of the tactical teams checked their gear, their faces set in grim determination under the glow of streetlights. Today, Detective Ian Mercer and Detective Sarah Langley's meticulously planned operation was set in motion, aimed at dismantling the last strongholds of Adrian Wolfe's criminal network.

The first raid targeted a suburban mansion, reputedly a luxurious facade for the darkest of Wolfe's dealings. As the clock struck 3 AM, Alpha Team moved silently through the shadows, their movements precise. The breach was initiated with a swift, controlled explosion that opened the front door without causing widespread damage. The team entered in a fluid, practiced motion, room-clearing procedures executed with professional calm.

Simultaneously, across town, Beta Team approached an industrial warehouse that served as a storage site for Wolfe's illicit materials. Drones hovered overhead, providing live feed to the command center where Ian and Sarah monitored the progress of each team. The warehouse, surrounded by a high fence topped with barbed wire, presented a more formidable physical challenge. The tactical unit used bolt cutters and grappling hooks, overcoming obstacles with methodical efficiency.

At another critical location, a hidden underground club where the elite gathered to partake in Wolfe's psychological games, Gamma Team used a more covert approach. Disguised in plain sight, they blended with the night shift workers until they were close enough to secure entry points, allowing additional forces to enter and secure the premises with minimal alert to the patrons inside.

Each raid was underpinned by strict orders to prioritize evidence collection and minimize conflict. As teams swept through buildings, they gathered computers, documents, and other crucial evidence, tagging and bagging anything that could later substantiate the legal case against Wolfe and his associates.

Back at the command center, Ian watched the progress with an intense focus. The success of this operation was crucial not just for the case but for restoring peace to Willow's End. He communicated quietly with team leaders, providing guidance and making decisions on resource allocation as reports came in.

Sarah, meanwhile, coordinated with the forensic units, ensuring that evidence from the raids was handled correctly to prevent any chain-of-custody issues that could jeopardize their admissibility in court. Her attention to detail ensured that all collected materials were meticulously documented.

As the night progressed, the raids continued with relentless efficiency. At Ian's direction, locations were secured, suspects were detained, and no casualties were reported. The precision of the operations spoke to the countless hours of preparation and training that the teams had undergone.

Towards the dawn, as the first hints of light began to dispel the darkness, the scale of their success became apparent. Over two dozen high-ranking members of Wolfe's organization were in custody, and significant quantities of incriminating evidence were en route to secure evidence processing facilities.

Ian allowed himself a moment of quiet satisfaction as he and Sarah reviewed the initial reports. Their strategy had worked; Wolfe's network was effectively crippled, its operations exposed and its leaders captured.

However, the morning's first light also brought a palpable sense of anticipation for what was to come. With the raids completed, the real work would begin—sifting through the evidence, interrogating suspects, and preparing for the trials that would surely be a spectacle in the legal and public arenas.

The chapter closed on a scene of controlled chaos at the precinct, where officers and detectives bustled about, energized by their night's work and the prospect of finally turning the tide against the corruption that had seeped into their town. While there was much to do, for the first time in a long time, there was a collective feeling of hope—an end was in sight, and it was largely thanks to the relentless efforts of Ian and Sarah.

After the successful execution of the coordinated raids, the evidence processing phase began. Ian Mercer and Sarah Langley, along with their team of forensic experts and analysts, convened in the evidence room, which was now filled with boxes of documents, hard drives, and other digital media seized during the raids. The room buzzed with the sound of machinery and low conversations as each piece of evidence was catalogued and examined.

Ian, overseeing the operation, approached Sarah, who was scrutinizing a series of financial documents spread out on a large table. "Find anything interesting?" he asked, his voice hopeful.

Sarah looked up, her eyes reflecting both fatigue and excitement. "Yes, actually. These financial statements show a series of transactions that don't just link back to Wolfe but also to several high-profile community members. It looks like we've got more than just a criminal network; we've got a full-blown syndicate with ties to the town's elite."

Ian's interest piqued, and he leaned in closer to examine the documents. "Can we prove these transactions are illicit?"

"We're piecing it together now," Sarah replied, pointing to a spreadsheet on her laptop. "See here? These are payments made out to shell companies, and from there, money was funneled into various accounts owned by our suspects. It's a classic money laundering setup."

Just then, an analyst, Jenna, approached them with a hard drive in her hand. "Detectives, you might want to take a look at this. We've managed to decrypt emails from this drive that reference several of the transactions Sarah is tracking."

Ian and Sarah moved to a computer where Jenna had uploaded the contents of the drive. As they scrolled through the emails, the depth of the conspiracy began to unfold before their eyes.

"Look at this," Ian pointed out, stopping at a particularly incriminating email thread. "This confirms that Wolfe was not just a participant but the orchestrator. He's directing the flow of money and also dictating how the funds should be used."

Sarah nodded, absorbing the details. "And here, these emails between Wolfe and Mayor Voss—looks like the Mayor was not only aware of the operations but may have been benefiting from them directly."

The gravity of their discovery was not lost on them. Ian rubbed his chin, deep in thought. "We need to document every piece of this conversation. It could be key in the trials."

As the morning progressed, more connections were discovered. Another team member, Mark, called them over to another table where a series of photographs were laid out. "These were found in a locked safe in Wolfe's office. They're not just any photos; these are surveillance shots of various high-ranking officials in compromising positions."

"Blackmail," Sarah concluded, a chill running down her spine. "Wolfe was keeping insurance."

Ian sighed, the weight of their findings heavy on his shoulders. "This is bigger than we thought. Wolfe had his hands in everything, manipulating not just money, but people—powerful people."

Sarah, looking determined, began organizing the photographs and documents into evidence folders. "We're going to need more than just our team on this. It's time to bring in the DA, and perhaps the FBI. This is no longer just a local crime."

Ian agreed, his resolve hardening. "Let's get everything we have over to the DA. We need to move fast now that we know how deep this goes."

As they prepared to leave the evidence room, Ian stopped and looked back at the tables covered with evidence. "We knew Wolfe was dangerous, but this..." he shook his head, "this is a level of corruption that's going to shake our town to its core."

Sarah placed a reassuring hand on his arm. "We'll get through this, Ian. Together."

The chapter closed with Ian and Sarah walking out of the evidence room, their silhouettes passing through the light spilling from the doorway, ready to face whatever challenges lay ahead with a new understanding of the scale of their adversary's reach. The fight was far from over, but they were more equipped than ever to take it on.

The aftermath of the coordinated raids rippled through Willow's End as dawn broke over the horizon. News of the operation spread quickly, igniting a firestorm of media coverage and public scrutiny. In the heart of this whirlwind, Detectives Ian Mercer and Sarah Langley worked tirelessly to consolidate their gains against Adrian Wolfe's network.

In the precinct's operations center, Ian and Sarah reviewed the latest updates from their teams. The successful raids had yielded not only crucial evidence but had significantly disrupted Wolfe's operations.

Several of his key lieutenants had been detained, and many of his illicit assets were now under police control.

"Looks like we've managed to freeze his financial assets effectively," Ian noted, examining the financial reports flashing on the screen. "Without access to his funds, Wolfe's ability to operate is severely hampered."

Sarah, who was coordinating with the legal team, added, "And with the amount of evidence we've collected, we're in a strong position to push for maximum charges. This is a significant blow to his organization."

As they strategized their next moves, a junior detective approached with a stack of preliminary interrogation reports. "Sir, ma'am, these are the initial statements from the suspects we brought in. Several are willing to testify against Wolfe in exchange for plea deals."

Ian scanned the documents, a sense of satisfaction evident in his expression. "Good work. Let's use this momentum. Every piece of testimony adds another layer to our case."

Outside the precinct, the public reaction was a mixture of shock and relief. Local news outlets swarmed the area, broadcasting live updates and interviewing residents shaken by the revelations. The community's unrest was palpable, but so was their support for the ongoing police efforts.

"We need to address the media. It's important to reassure the public that we're taking all necessary steps to ensure their safety," Sarah suggested, looking out the window at the gathering crowd of reporters.

Ian agreed, "Absolutely. Let's prepare a statement. It's crucial that we communicate transparency and control."

Later that day, Ian stood before a bank of microphones, Sarah by his side, as he addressed the gathered press. "Today's operations have dealt a significant blow to a criminal network that has plagued our community for far too long," he declared, his voice steady and authoritative. "We have arrested key individuals and seized assets that were instrumental in their operations. Our investigation continues, but let me be clear: we will not rest until every person involved is brought to justice."

The press conference was brief but effective. As Ian and Sarah walked back into the precinct, they were met with nods of approval from their colleagues. The atmosphere in the office was buoyant; the successful raids had boosted the morale of the entire department.

Back in their makeshift war room, Ian and Sarah discussed their next steps. "We've got Wolfe on the back foot now. We need to keep the pressure on, dig into every connection we've uncovered," Ian stated, his focus already shifting to the next phase of their operation.

Sarah, pulling up a list of potential leads on her laptop, agreed. "I'll coordinate with the federal agencies and see if they can expedite the processing of the digital evidence. The quicker we get the data, the faster we can move."

As the day wound down, Ian took a moment to reflect on the progress they had made. The operation had taken a toll on him, both physically and mentally, but seeing the tangible results of their hard work reaffirmed his commitment to the cause.

The chapter closed with Ian looking out over the town from his office window, the early evening light casting long shadows across the streets. Despite the victory today, he knew the battle was far from over. But for now, Willow's End was a little safer, a little closer to breaking free from the shadows that had long ensnared it.

As the dust settled from the day's successful raids, Ian Mercer and Sarah Langley took a moment to debrief in Ian's office, surrounded by the tangible results of their hard work: stacks of evidence files, digital records, and intercepted communications. They were joined by Agent Ramirez, who had been instrumental in coordinating the federal resources for the operation.

"Well, you two certainly pulled off a significant victory today," Agent Ramirez began, her tone both congratulatory and serious. "We've been analyzing the encrypted data from the raids, and it's clear that Wolfe's network was even more extensive than we feared."

Ian, leaning back in his chair, rubbed his temples. "The deeper we dig, the more unsettling it becomes. But today, we've made real progress. Sarah, the evidence you organized was key."

Sarah, who was scrolling through a digital file on her tablet, looked up. "It's shocking, really. Some of the communications we've uncovered show just how manipulative Wolfe was. He wasn't just a criminal; he was a puppet master."

Agent Ramirez added, "Indeed. And our analysts are still piecing together some of the financial trails. But I wanted to discuss what comes next. With Wolfe's assets frozen and his allies turning on him, we expect him to make a desperate move soon."

Ian nodded, his mind already racing with potential scenarios. "We need to anticipate his strategies. Historically, he's always had a contingency plan. Sarah, we should review all his known associates again, see if we can predict his next step."

Sarah agreed, her expression focused. "Absolutely. I'll start compiling a list of all the secondary connections. We might find a pattern or a weak link."

The conversation shifted as Ian turned to Agent Ramirez. "I appreciate all the support from your team, Agent Ramirez. This case has grown beyond what any of us expected, and your expertise has been invaluable."

Agent Ramirez smiled slightly. "It's been a collaborative effort, Ian. Your team's dedication has been the driving force here."

As they spoke, Ian reflected on the personal toll the case had taken. "You know, when we started this investigation, I didn't realize how much it would consume us. It's more than just a job now—it's personal."

Sarah listened intently, then responded, "It is personal, Ian. But think about the difference we're making. We're not just solving a case; we're cleaning up our town, protecting future generations from Wolfe's influence."

Ian considered her words, a sense of responsibility settling over him. "You're right, Sarah. It's about the bigger picture. And personally, I've learned a lot about myself through this—about resilience and trust."

Sarah leaned forward, her voice earnest. "And I've learned a lot from you, Ian. About courage, about pushing through even when things seem impossible."

Their discussion was interrupted by a notification on Ian's computer. A new message had come in—a tip about a possible location where Wolfe might be trying to regroup. Ian's focus sharpened instantly.

"Looks like we've got a new lead," he announced, turning the screen so both Sarah and Agent Ramirez could see. "Wolfe might be down, but he's not out. We've got to act on this quickly."

Agent Ramirez stood, ready to mobilize her team. "Let's get on it then. The sooner we catch him, the sooner we can put an end to this."

As they left Ian's office to prepare for the next phase of their operation, the weight of their responsibilities remained, tempered by the growth they had experienced and the bonds they had strengthened. The revelations of the day had reshaped their understanding of the case and of each other, driving them forward with renewed determination and a deeper commitment to their cause.

The chapter closed with Ian and Sarah stepping into the bustling operations center, ready to lead their teams into whatever challenges lay ahead. Their journey was far from over, but each victory brought them closer to the resolution they sought.

Chapter 13
The Setup

In the secure confines of the Willow's End Police Department's strategy room, Detective Ian Mercer, Detective Sarah Langley, and a select group of tactical advisors, including Agent Ramirez, gathered around a large digital map projected on the wall. The atmosphere was thick with anticipation as they prepared to outline the final confrontation with Adrian Wolfe.

Ian started the meeting with a firm tone, "We've got Wolfe on the ropes, but he's not out yet. This final confrontation needs to be tight and decisive. We can't afford any slip-ups."

Sarah, her eyes fixed on the map, nodded in agreement. "Based on the latest intelligence, we believe Wolfe might try to regroup at the old mill on the outskirts of town. It's isolated enough for him to feel secure, yet accessible enough for a quick escape."

Agent Ramirez, who had been coordinating the federal support, chimed in, "Our satellite surveillance supports that. We've noticed increased activity in that area, suggesting that Wolfe might be consolidating resources there."

Ian pointed at the map, indicating the routes leading to the mill. "We'll need to cut off all possible escape routes. I propose we set up roadblocks here, here, and here. We'll also need aerial surveillance to track any movement in or out of the area."

Sarah highlighted another aspect of their strategy. "We should consider Wolfe's likely countermeasures. He knows we're coming, so he'll be prepared. I suggest we use decoys to mislead him about our actual point of entry."

"That's a good point, Sarah," Ian responded, marking potential decoy routes on the map. "We can deploy two teams as decoys on the north and west approaches. The real strike team will approach from the south where the cover is thickest."

Agent Ramirez added, "I'll arrange for the decoy teams to have full federal support, including armored vehicles and aerial decoys. It should give Wolfe enough to focus on while you make the real move."

The tactical advisors, experienced in urban and rural operations, began discussing the specifics of the entry tactics. "Considering the layout of the mill and the surrounding area, I recommend using smoke as cover for the entry. It'll help obscure the team's movements and minimize our exposure," one advisor suggested.

Ian considered the recommendation thoughtfully. "Let's include IR strobes on all our operatives. Smoke or no, we need to keep track of everyone once inside."

Sarah, always attentive to detail, brought up communication protocols. "Let's run a full check on all communication equipment tonight. Last thing we need is a blackout in the middle of the operation."

"Agreed," Ian affirmed, making a note. "Also, let's have medical teams on standby, just in case. This could get messy, and I want quick extraction for anyone injured."

As the meeting drew to a close, Ian looked around the room, meeting the eyes of each team member. "This is it, the moment we've been working towards. We've all put a lot into this case, and I know it's been tough on everyone. But we're close now. Let's keep focused, follow the plan, and bring Wolfe down for good."

Sarah added a final word of encouragement, "We've got this, team. Let's bring some peace back to Willow's End."

The meeting disbanded with team members moving into their respective preparatory tasks. Ian and Sarah lingered for a moment, reviewing the details on the digital map, their expressions a mix of resolve and the weight of the responsibility they shouldered.

As they left the strategy room, their steps were measured, their minds already running through the scenarios that would unfold in the hours to come. The chapter closed with the setting sun casting long shadows through the windows, symbolizing the looming confrontation that would either end Wolfe's reign of terror or plunge Willow's End further into chaos.

As the early morning mist clung to the ground, shrouding the old mill in a ghostly veil, the tactical teams were in place, hidden in the shadows, their movements as silent as the breeze whispering through the leaves. The plan had been meticulously set, every potential contingency considered. Yet, unbeknownst to Ian Mercer and Sarah Langley, Adrian Wolfe had not been idle.

Deep within the confines of the mill, Wolfe was well-prepared for the impending confrontation. He had always prided himself on being several steps ahead of his adversaries, and this time was no different. Surveillance equipment hummed softly in the background, screens flickering with feeds from cameras hidden around the perimeter of the mill. Wolfe watched, a thin smile playing across his lips as he observed the police forces encircling his stronghold.

His countermove was simple yet cunning. Knowing that his communications might be monitored, he had planted misinformation— a deliberate leak to throw the police off. Earlier communications indicated that he was gathering a large force at the mill to make a stand. In reality, Wolfe had already evacuated the most critical members of his network to a secondary location days before, leaving behind only a small contingent to maintain appearances.

Wolfe's true plan involved a remote operation. In a secure room, his technical team was initiating a series of cyber-attacks aimed at disrupting police communications and sowing confusion among the tactical teams.

As the first signs of dawn broke, the attacks began, targeting the police's mobile data terminals and the command center's mainframe.

Back at the police command center, the first signs of trouble appeared abruptly. Screens flickered and went dark, radios crackled with static, and the officers faced sudden blackouts in their communication network. Ian and Sarah, positioned in a mobile command vehicle, quickly realized that they were experiencing a coordinated cyber-assault.

"Damn it, Wolfe is hitting our systems," Ian cursed under his breath as he tried to re-establish connections.

Sarah, maintaining her composure amidst the chaos, coordinated with the IT specialists on site. "We need to switch to the backup comms now. Get those emergency protocols running!"

As the police scrambled to mitigate the cyber-attacks, Wolfe executed the next phase of his plan. A small convoy of vehicles, previously hidden in the mill's underground garage, made a swift exit through a back route that was less guarded. The convoy carried Wolfe and his closest associates, slipping away just as the tactical teams began to realize the diversion.

Meanwhile, the teams at the mill faced little resistance, capturing only a handful of operatives who seemed almost too willing to surrender. It soon became clear that Wolfe's main force was never there. The realization hit Ian and Sarah hard as they regrouped to assess the situation.

"We've been played," Ian admitted, frustration evident in his voice. "He knew we were coming and planned this from the start."

Sarah, analyzing the map, pointed to a potential route Wolfe might have taken. "He's not far ahead, and this area is still heavily wooded. We can deploy aerial surveillance and try to catch up with him."

Rapidly adjusting their strategy, Ian coordinated with the aerial units to track the fleeing convoy. Every available unit was redirected to pursue Wolfe, the chase intensifying as the sun climbed higher in the sky.

As the chapter closed, Ian and Sarah were back in the command vehicle, the screens now stabilized and displaying live feeds from the pursuing units. The chase was on, the morning's calm shattered by the urgent roar of engines and the distant thump of helicopter blades. The battle of wits with Wolfe was reaching its climax, each move and countermove bringing them closer to a final confrontation.

In the aftermath of the botched raid and the ensuing chase, tensions within Ian Mercer and Sarah Langley's team escalated as they regrouped at the command center. The atmosphere was thick with frustration and fatigue as they faced the reality of Adrian Wolfe's successful evasion.

"I can't believe he slipped through again!" Detective Mason, one of the tactical team leaders, slammed a fist down on the table. His team had been one of the first into the mill, and his frustration was palpable.

Ian, who had been silently reviewing the latest updates on Wolfe's movements, looked up, his expression somber. "It's not just you, Mason. We all walked into his trap. He planned this meticulously."

Sarah tried to soothe the rising tempers. "Let's focus on what we can do next, not what went wrong. We know Wolfe is heading west; aerial surveillance has him in sight."

Agent Ramirez, who had been coordinating with federal units, chimed in, supporting Sarah's call for focus. "Sarah's right. We need to coordinate our next steps carefully. Wolfe is desperate, which makes him dangerous but also prone to mistakes."

"But how did he know exactly when to hit us?" another agent, Lila, asked, her voice tinged with suspicion. "Could there be a leak on our team?"

The suggestion hung in the air, heavy and uncomfortable. Ian's gaze swept over the group, his mind racing with the same worry. "It's a possibility we can't ignore. We need to review all communications and access to our plans immediately."

Sarah, sensing the growing mistrust, stepped in firmly. "Let's not jump to conclusions. Wolfe is a master manipulator; he doesn't need a mole to anticipate our moves. He knows how we think because we've been chasing him for so long."

Mason rubbed his forehead, clearly exhausted. "So, what's the plan now? We keep chasing shadows until he decides to disappear for good?"

"No," Ian responded decisively. "We tighten our circle. We limit information flow to essential personnel only. And we push harder. Wolfe is running out of options."

Ramirez, who had been quietly making notes, looked up. "We also need to think about protecting ourselves legally. Wolfe will use any missteps we make against us. Every move from now on has to be by the book."

Sarah nodded in agreement. "Absolutely. Let's ensure all our warrants are solid and our evidence chain is unbreakable. We can't give him any room to maneuver."

The team fell silent, each member processing the situation and their role in it. Finally, Ian stood, his stance resolute. "This team has been through a lot. We've faced setbacks before, and we've always come out stronger. Wolfe thinks he's steering this game, but he's mistaken. We're ending this on our terms."

Mason looked up, his expression shifting from frustration to determination. "You're right, Ian. We're all in this together. Let's bring this guy down."

Sarah smiled slightly, her confidence unshaken. "That's the spirit. Let's use every resource we have, every ally we can muster. Wolfe's network is crumbling, and he knows it."

As the team members began to focus on their specific tasks, the tension that had filled the room started to dissipate, replaced by a renewed sense of purpose. Each member knew their part, each understood the stakes, and each was committed to ending Wolfe's reign of terror.

As they dispersed to carry out their roles, Ian and Sarah lingered for a moment, their partnership strengthened in the face of adversity. "We've got a tough road ahead," Ian remarked quietly.

Sarah nodded, her gaze steady. "Yes, but it's one we'll travel together. Let's catch Wolfe and end this."

The chapter closed with the team re-energized, moving forward with a unified front, their resolve hardened and their mission clear. Wolfe's countermove had been a blow, but it was not a defeat. It was a call to action that they answered with unwavering determination.

In a hastily arranged war room within the precinct, Detective Ian Mercer and Detective Sarah Langley worked alongside their tactical team to finalize preparations for the anticipated showdown with Adrian Wolfe. Maps and surveillance images were displayed prominently, showing the rugged terrain around the old mill and potential locations where Wolfe might make his last stand.

Ian, looking over the latest aerial photos, pointed to a secluded area. "Here, this is where we think he's heading. It's remote, hard to access with vehicles, which is exactly why he would choose it."

Sarah, coordinating with the communications team, added, "We have the satellite phones ready, ensuring we won't lose contact this time. Wolfe won't get another chance to use our tech against us."

Agent Ramirez, liaising with federal support units, joined the conversation. "I've got confirmation that the FBI's tactical unit will be in position by 0600 hours. They'll be our eyes in the sky until you're on the ground."

Ian nodded in approval before addressing the entire room. "Listen up, everyone. This is where we stop playing defense. Wolfe thinks he's leading this dance, but he's about to find out he's sorely mistaken. We're going to cut him off and close in before he has a chance to realize we've changed the game."

Sarah, looking over personnel files, spoke up. "I've assigned team leaders for each entry point. We're using a pincer movement to box him in. No more chases after today."

A tactical advisor, Captain Moreno, raised a concern. "We need to consider Wolfe's likely defenses. He knows the terrain better than anyone. There could be booby traps, or worse."

"I've thought of that," Ian replied. "That's why we're sending in drones first. We'll have a full sweep of the area before any boots hit the ground. Safety is our top priority."

Sarah continued, focusing on the broader strategy. "Once we have Wolfe contained, we need to communicate with him. Try to get him to surrender peacefully. It's a long shot, but if we can avoid gunfire, we should."

"Agreed," Ian said, looking to Agent Ramirez. "Can we set up a negotiation team on standby?"

"Already done," Ramirez confirmed. "We'll have experienced negotiators ready to talk him down. But they'll only move in on your signal."

As they worked through the details, the room filled with a focused energy. Each member of the team understood their role and the part they played in this carefully choreographed operation.

Ian took a moment to step aside with Sarah, lowering his voice. "You ready for this, Sarah? After today, things could change for us."

Sarah met his gaze squarely. "I'm ready. After all we've been through, I want nothing more than to see this through. To finally put an end to Wolfe's games."

Ian smiled, the bond between them stronger than ever. "Me too. Let's do this right. For the town, for the victims, and for ourselves."

The preparations continued into the night, with every detail scrutinized and every contingency planned for. As the team members dispersed to grab a few hours of rest before the operation, Ian and Sarah stayed behind, reviewing every step one last time.

The chapter closed not with a sense of foreboding, but with a palpable determination. In the quiet of the empty war room, Ian and Sarah shared a quiet resolve. Tomorrow would bring a confrontation long in the making, and they were ready to face it head-on, confident in their plan, their team, and each other.

Chapter 14
The Confrontation

As dawn tinged the sky with shades of gray and pink, the Willow's End Police Department was a hive of activity. Today was the day they would confront Adrian Wolfe, and the air was charged with a tense anticipation. Detective Ian Mercer and Detective Sarah Langley were at the heart of the preparations, overseeing the final checks on equipment and personnel.

In the precinct's garage, Ian reviewed the array of tactical vehicles lined up for deployment. Each SUV was equipped with reinforced armor, and the trunks were open, displaying an arsenal of non-lethal weapons designed to ensure a controlled confrontation.

"Make sure every unit has tear gas and stun grenades. I want options that don't involve live ammunition unless absolutely necessary," Ian instructed a group of officers, who nodded and double-checked their gear.

Sarah, meanwhile, was in the communications center setting up secure lines. "Let's run through the signal checklist one more time," she said to the communications officer. "I want confirmation that all channels are encrypted and operational."

The officer flicked through several screens, verifying each one. "All systems green, Detective Langley. We have satellite and drone feeds live and recording."

Outside, Agent Ramirez coordinated with the federal units. "Positions will be synced to GPS tags on each team member. We'll have real-time tracking on everyone in the field," she explained over the radio.

Ian joined Sarah, updating her on the arsenal preparations. "How are the comms looking?"

"Solid," Sarah replied. "We have multiple backups in place. If Wolfe tries to jam us again, he'll find it much harder this time."

As they talked, Captain Moreno approached, holding a tablet with a live drone feed. "Here's the latest aerial recon. Wolfe's forces appear to be fortifying the north side of the mill. Looks like he expects us to come from that direction."

Ian studied the feed, noting the positions of Wolfe's men. "He's still playing chess, but we're three moves ahead. We'll approach from the south and east, split his focus."

"Do the teams know about the change in entry points?" Sarah asked, her brow furrowed with concern.

"Yes, I briefed them an hour ago. Everyone's prepped and ready to adapt to on-the-fly changes," Moreno confirmed.

Ian gave a curt nod, satisfied. "Good. What's the ETA on the federal tactical support?"

"They're en route, should be in position within the hour," Ramirez reported, joining the group.

"We'll start moving out shortly. Let's get everyone briefed on the latest intel and ensure they're ready to move on my command," Ian directed, his tone leaving no room for doubt.

The group dispersed to carry out their final tasks, each member focused and alert. As they prepared to leave, Sarah caught up with Ian, her expression serious.

"This is it, Ian. You ready for this?"

Ian looked at her, his face set with determination. "As ready as we'll ever be. Let's end this."

The chapter closed with the team members loading into their vehicles, the first rays of sunlight breaking over the horizon, casting long shadows across the assembled force. It was a moment of calm before the storm, the silence a stark contrast to the chaos that would soon unfold.

As the police and federal units took their positions around the old mill, a silence settled over the area, punctuated only by the distant hum of drones and the occasional crackle of radio static. The tension was palpable; every officer knew that the confrontation with Adrian Wolfe was imminent.

Then, a black SUV appeared from the dense forest surrounding the mill, its approach slow and deliberate. As it came to a halt, the doors opened, and Adrian Wolfe stepped out, flanked by two of his most trusted lieutenants. His appearance was calm, almost defiant, as he surveyed the semi-circle of law enforcement encircling him.

Wolfe raised his hands slightly, showing he was unarmed, and then spoke, his voice carrying clearly in the quiet morning air. "Detective Mercer, Detective Langley, I must admit, I'm impressed. Not many could have coordinated such a formidable response."

Ian, standing behind a cover with Sarah, responded via loudspeaker, maintaining a safe distance. "Wolfe, this ends today. You have nowhere to go. Surrender now, and we can guarantee your safety."

Wolfe chuckled, shaking his head slightly. "Ian, after all these years, you still believe this is about escaping? No, I came here today to speak, to explain why I did what I did. You deserve that much, at least."

Sarah, skeptical, interjected. "There's nothing you can say that will justify your actions, Wolfe. You manipulated and hurt countless people."

Wolfe nodded, acknowledging her point. "True, my methods were... extreme. But my goal was to highlight the fragility of our societal structures, the ease with which people can be swayed, controlled. I forced people to confront the reality of their existence, the illusions they cling to."

Ian's voice was firm, his patience thinning. "You used fear and violence to make your point. You're not a philosopher, Wolfe; you're a terrorist."

Wolfe sighed, his expression one of resignation. "Perhaps. But consider this: my 'experiments' revealed truths that many spend lifetimes ignoring. Without my intervention, how long would those corruptions have continued unchecked? How many more victims would there have been of a more subtle, but equally destructive, nature?"

Sarah countered quickly, her tone laced with anger. "You don't get to decide how people confront their truths, Wolfe. You took away their choice, their freedom."

Wolfe spread his hands, as if in offering. "And now you'll take away mine. Fair enough. But remember, the ideas I've planted, the doubts I've sown about the integrity of those in power—they won't disappear with me."

Ian, ready to end the philosophical debate, gave a hand signal to the surrounding teams. "This is your last chance, Wolfe. Surrender, or we will take you by force."

Wolfe glanced around at the armed officers, a thin smile on his lips. "Force then. It seems fitting that this ends where it began, with a show of power. But know this, Detective Mercer, Detective Langley: my arrest will not heal the divisions I've exposed. Only understanding and change can do that."

As Wolfe finished his speech, he slowly lowered his hands, and in a swift motion that surprised everyone, he reached inside his jacket. The officers, perceiving a threat, reacted instinctively.

"Stand down, Wolfe!" Ian's command was sharp, echoing across the open field, as the situation teetered on the edge of violence.

Wolfe paused, his hand half-inside his jacket, a sardonic grin on his face. "A dramatic end, then?"

Before the situation could escalate further, Sarah, her voice calm but commanding, intervened. "Wolfe, don't do this. End it peacefully. You've made your point."

After a tense moment, Wolfe slowly withdrew his hand, empty, and raised both hands in the air, signaling his surrender. "Very well, Detective Langley. I yield."

The chapter closed with Wolfe stepping forward, the early morning light casting long shadows across the ground, as he moved to surrender himself to Ian and Sarah. The confrontation had reached its peak, and though Wolfe was in custody, the echoes of his unsettling philosophy lingered in the air, challenging everyone present to ponder the deeper implications of his actions.

As Adrian Wolfe walked forward, his hands raised in apparent surrender, the tension among the assembled law enforcement personnel did not ease. Detective Ian Mercer and Detective Sarah Langley exchanged a quick, wary glance, both sensing that the situation might still not be as it appeared.

As Wolfe approached, Ian instructed firmly, "Stop there, Wolfe. On your knees, hands on your head."

Wolfe complied, but his voice carried a tone of mocking compliance as he knelt. "As you wish, Detective. But you should know, I'm not without my precautions."

Sarah, maintaining a cautious distance, spoke into her radio. "All units, stay alert. He might have another trick up his sleeve."

No sooner had she finished speaking than a sharp, piercing sound echoed through the area—a high-pitched whine that seemed to come from several directions at once. Simultaneously, the ground a few yards away from where Wolfe knelt erupted, a cloud of smoke and debris mushrooming into the air.

"Back! Everyone, get back!" Ian shouted, realizing too late that Wolfe had laid a trap. The explosion was followed by a series of smaller blasts, cleverly designed to create chaos and provide Wolfe with a diversion.

In the ensuing confusion, Wolfe sprang to his feet and dashed towards a nearby thicket. The tactical teams, momentarily stunned, quickly regrouped and pursued him, their earlier caution giving way to urgent action.

Sarah, directing the response, yelled into her radio, "Tango team, flank left! Echo team, secure the perimeter. He won't get far!"

As the officers moved into action, Ian pursued Wolfe, navigating the dense smoke and debris. "Wolfe, it's over! Stop!"

From ahead, Wolfe's voice taunted back, "It's never over, Mercer! You should know that by now!"

Emerging from the smoke, Wolfe seemed to be heading towards a previously unseen escape route, likely another part of his elaborate contingency plans. Ian, his training kicking in, managed to close the distance, tackling Wolfe to the ground just as he was about to disappear into a hidden tunnel entrance.

As they struggled on the ground, Sarah caught up, her weapon drawn and aimed at Wolfe. "Enough, Wolfe! It ends here!"

Breathing heavily, Wolfe ceased struggling and laughed breathlessly. "Detective Langley, always so dramatic. Go on then, do what you must."

Ian, keeping Wolfe pinned down, looked up at Sarah. "Secure him. I'll check the tunnel for any more surprises."

Sarah nodded, handcuffing Wolfe while keeping her weapon trained on him. "You're under arrest, Wolfe. Anything you do from this point can and will be used against you in a court of law."

Wolfe, now subdued, smirked. "Ah, the formalities. But tell me, detectives, was it worth it? The chase, the game? Have you really won?"

Ian, returning from a quick sweep of the tunnel, confirmed it was clear. "We've won enough. You're in custody, and your network is dismantled."

Sarah, looking down at Wolfe, added, "You wanted to expose truths, Wolfe. Now it's your turn to face them."

As additional units arrived to secure Wolfe and search the area for any further hazards, the adrenaline began to subside, replaced by a weary satisfaction.

The chapter closed with Wolfe secured in a vehicle, ready for transport, and Ian and Sarah watching as the sun rose fully over the horizon, casting light on the chaos of the morning's events. Despite Wolfe's games and philosophical taunts, they had upheld their duty, protecting the community from one man's dangerous vision. The confrontation had tested them to their limits, but they emerged resolute and ready to face whatever challenges lay ahead.

As Adrian Wolfe was secured in the back of a patrol car, his eyes flickered with an unreadable intensity. Detectives Ian Mercer and Sarah Langley stood outside the vehicle, watching closely, both aware that until Wolfe was behind bars at the precinct, the operation wasn't truly over.

"Do you think he has more surprises planned?" Sarah whispered, her eyes never leaving Wolfe.

Ian, who was overseeing the final checks and communicating with the other teams via radio, nodded slightly. "It's Wolfe. I wouldn't put it past him to have a plan B, C, and D."

Inside the car, Wolfe leaned towards the mesh that separated him from the front seats, his voice calm. "Detective Mercer, Detective Langley, do you truly believe this is the end?"

Ian ignored him, focusing on his radio. "Echo team, status report?"

Before the team could respond, a loud crash echoed through the area. The vehicle holding Wolfe shook violently as if struck by a massive force. In a blink, one side of the car was ripped open, metal twisting and sparks flying.

Sarah and Ian whipped around, guns drawn, as masked figures emerged from the surrounding woods. It was a rescue operation—Wolfe's loyalists attempting a daring daylight extraction.

"Get down!" Ian shouted, pulling Sarah to cover behind another vehicle as bullets began to fly.

Wolfe, seizing the moment, kicked at the car door, widening the gap created by the explosion. He scrambled out, a smug smile visible even in the chaos.

Sarah fired towards the attackers, providing cover as Ian called for backup. "We need reinforcements at the west perimeter! Suspect is attempting escape!"

As Ian provided covering fire, Sarah tried to flank the attackers, moving swiftly and low. "Wolfe! It's not too late to stop this!"

Wolfe, now partially free, shouted back amid the gunfire, "Freedom, Detective Langley, is always worth pursuing!"

The skirmish was intense but brief. Wolfe's rescuers, heavily armed and professional, laid down suppressing fire, slowly edging towards Wolfe's position.

Ian, realizing they were outnumbered and outgunned, made a quick decision. "Sarah, fall back! We need to regroup!"

Reluctantly, Sarah complied, and they retreated to a safer distance, watching helplessly as Wolfe and his rescuers disappeared into the woods.

Once they reached safety, Ian slammed his fist against the side of the car. "Damn it! He planned this from the start."

Sarah, catching her breath, was quick to respond. "We can track them. They can't have gone far."

Ian was already on his radio. "All units, track and follow! He's heading northeast, towards the river. Set up a perimeter and wait for my signal to close in."

As backup arrived and the immediate danger subsided, Ian and Sarah coordinated a rapid response, setting up surveillance drones and calling in additional resources.

"We'll get him, Sarah. He won't get far," Ian assured her, though his expression showed his frustration.

Sarah nodded, reloading her weapon and preparing for the next phase of the pursuit. "Let's finish this. For good this time."

The chapter closed with the sounds of sirens and helicopters in the distance, the early morning calm shattered by the unexpected violence. Ian and Sarah, determined and focused, led their teams deeper into the forest, following the trail left by Wolfe and his rescuers. The direct confrontation might have ended, but the chase was far from over.

Chapter 15
Reflections

The forest was quiet again, the chaos of the earlier confrontation fading into a tense silence that settled over the area like a heavy blanket. Detective Ian Mercer and Detective Sarah Langley, along with a few members of their tactical team, stood around the clearing where Adrian Wolfe had made his last, unsuccessful bid for freedom. The ground was littered with evidence of the struggle: discarded weapons, trampled underbrush, and deep tire tracks that marred the earth.

Sarah, her brow furrowed with concentration, was busy coordinating with the forensics team. "Make sure to document everything. I want photos, I want samples, I want everything we can use to track them down."

Ian, standing a few feet away, was on the phone with command. "Yes, we're securing the scene now. Wolfe is still at large, but we're regrouping and setting up a new perimeter. He won't get far."

As he hung up, he turned to Sarah. "How are you holding up?"

Sarah sighed, tucking a loose strand of hair behind her ear. "Frustrated. We were so close, Ian. If we had just been a bit faster—"

Ian cut her off gently. "We did everything we could. Wolfe is cunning; he's always been one step ahead. But this time, we're closing that gap. He's running out of options."

A junior detective approached them, holding a tablet. "Detectives, we've picked up heat signatures heading north from the last known position. It looks like Wolfe and his team are heading towards the old quarry."

Ian nodded, his jaw set. "Good work. Relay that to all units. Sarah, let's move out. We need to keep the pressure on."

As they prepared to leave, Agent Ramirez joined them, her expression serious. "I just got off the line with the Director. He's sending additional resources. We have satellite coverage now; Wolfe won't be able to hide for long."

Sarah, checking her weapon and gear, looked determined. "Let's make sure of that. We can't let him slip through our fingers again."

The team moved out, their steps quick and purposeful. As they walked, Ian glanced over at Sarah. "You know, after all this is over, we're going to have to really look at how things went down. There'll be inquiries, investigations..."

Sarah nodded. "I know. And we'll be ready for them. We've done everything by the book, as much as Wolfe has tried to make us do otherwise."

Ian smiled wryly. "He's challenged us, that's for sure. Made us question a lot of what we thought we knew about law enforcement, about justice."

"Maybe that's a good thing," Sarah mused as they reached the edge of the clearing. "Maybe we needed to be pushed, to make sure we're really serving justice and not just going through the motions."

Ian looked thoughtful. "Maybe. But right now, my only concern is bringing Wolfe in. We can reflect on the philosophical implications later."

As they disappeared into the woods, the scene at the clearing continued to be processed by the forensics team. The aftermath of the confrontation was a stark reminder of the high stakes of their ongoing battle with Wolfe. Each piece of evidence collected was a piece of the puzzle, bringing them closer to capturing a man who had turned their world upside down.

The chapter closed not with a resolution, but with a renewed commitment to the chase. Ian and Sarah, leading their team deeper into the woods, were figures of resolve, their determination a clear signal that they would not stop until Adrian Wolfe was brought to justice, no matter what reflections that might later bring.

Back at the precinct, the atmosphere was charged with a mix of exhaustion and urgency. Detective Ian Mercer and Detective Sarah Langley sat in a debriefing room, surrounded by their core team, including tactical leaders and key investigative personnel. The walls were lined with screens showing live feeds and updates from various surveillance teams still in the field.

Commander Stevens, overseeing the operation, initiated the debrief. "Let's start with a status update. Where do we stand?"

Ian responded, his voice steady despite the fatigue evident in his eyes. "Wolfe is still at large, but we've significantly narrowed his potential escape routes. The quarry area is completely sealed off, and we have drones overhead keeping watch."

Sarah added, "Forensic teams are processing all the evidence collected from the last encounter. We have some of his men in custody, and they're being interrogated as we speak. We might get something useful from them yet."

Commander Stevens nodded, taking notes. "What about the public response? This operation has drawn a lot of attention."

Sarah glanced at the media liaison officer, who spoke up. "The press is all over this. We're managing the narrative carefully, emphasizing the danger Wolfe poses and our commitment to public safety. However, there's a lot of scrutiny on our methods, especially after the explosion near the mill."

Ian leaned forward, his expression serious. "We need to be transparent about our actions. Everything we've done has been within the legal parameters. Make sure that's communicated clearly."

The media liaison nodded. "Absolutely, Detective Mercer. We're preparing a press release with all the details, and we're planning a press conference for tomorrow morning."

Sarah looked around the room. "We also need to address the internal impact. This chase has taken a toll on our team. I want to make sure everyone has access to support services if they need it."

Commander Stevens agreed. "Good point, Detective Langley. I'll arrange for our psychological services to be on standby. We can't overlook the wellbeing of our own people."

The conversation shifted back to tactical considerations. "What's our next move?" Commander Stevens asked, looking towards Ian.

"We keep the pressure on," Ian stated firmly. "Wolfe is running out of options, and he knows it. Our best chance is to maintain our momentum and catch him before he can regroup."

Sarah chimed in, "I suggest we also re-examine all of Wolfe's known associates. There may be someone we missed, someone who could be helping him now."

Commander Stevens made a note. "I'll assign a team to review all connections immediately. Anything else we should be considering?"

Ian thought for a moment before responding. "Yes, we should prepare for the possibility that Wolfe might try to communicate with the public. He's always had a flair for the dramatic, and he might use this situation to spread his message."

"I'll alert our cyber units to monitor for any such attempts," the media liaison added quickly. "We'll intercept anything he tries to put out."

As the meeting drew to a close, Sarah summarized their stance. "We remain focused and ready. We've overcome his tricks before, and we'll do it again. Let's stay sharp and bring him in."

Commander Stevens concluded, "Thank you, everyone. Let's reconvene in four hours unless something urgent comes up sooner. Stay vigilant and keep communication lines open."

The team members dispersed, each returning to their respective duties with renewed determination. The chapter closed with Ian and Sarah pausing for a moment in the hallway, sharing a look of quiet resolve. They were in the midst of one of the toughest challenges of their careers, but they were not without support, both within the department and from the community they were striving to protect. The public response was mixed, but the mission was clear, and they were not backing down.

After the intense debrief, Detective Ian Mercer found himself in the quiet solitude of his office, the earlier adrenaline of the chase giving way to a more reflective mood. He sat at his desk, surrounded by case files and notes that told the story of their long pursuit of Adrian Wolfe. Each document was a reminder of the complexity of the case and the personal toll it had exacted not just on him but on his entire team.

Ian leaned back in his chair, his thoughts drifting to the many faces and events that had marked this ordeal. His partnership with Sarah, in particular, came to the forefront. Their relationship had been tested in countless ways, forged in the fire of this relentless pursuit. He realized just how much he relied on her strength and insight.

Meanwhile, Sarah Langley was in the small, somewhat neglected garden behind the precinct, a place she went when the weight of their responsibilities felt overwhelming. The cool air and the sound of rustling leaves provided a brief respite from the chaos. As she sat on a worn bench, she thought about the cost of their mission, the lines they had walked, and sometimes blurred, in their quest to bring Wolfe to justice.

Sarah's thoughts were interrupted by Ian's approach. He sat beside her, his presence a comforting reminder that she was not alone in this reflection.

"You okay?" Ian asked, his voice low and concerned.

Sarah looked over, managing a small smile. "Just thinking about everything. About Wolfe, about what he said. He's wrong, isn't he? About us?"

Ian nodded, his expression somber. "He is. Wolfe sees the world through his own distorted lens. He tries to justify his actions by painting everyone else as corrupt or blind. But we're not like him. We fight to protect, not to manipulate or control."

Sarah sighed, leaning back. "I know. It's just hard sometimes, seeing the lines get so blurred. This case has pushed us in ways I never expected."

Ian placed a reassuring hand on her shoulder. "It's pushed us, but it hasn't broken us. And it won't. We do this job not because it's easy, but because it's necessary. Because at the end of the day, we're the barrier between the chaos Wolfe wants and the order we strive to maintain."

Sarah turned to face him, her resolve firming. "You're right. And no matter how this ends, I know we've done our best, stayed true to our principles."

They sat in silence for a few moments, each lost in their thoughts, the quiet of the garden enveloping them. It was a necessary pause, a moment to gather strength.

Finally, Ian stood up, offering Sarah a hand. "Come on, we should get back. Wolfe is still out there, and we have a job to finish."

Sarah took his hand and stood, her determination clear. "Let's finish this. For the city, for our team, and for ourselves."

As they walked back to the building, the chapter closed on their shared resolve. The personal reflections and emotional reckonings they'd experienced were not just challenges to overcome but reminders of why they had chosen their path. They were ready to face whatever lay ahead, strengthened by their bond and their unyielding commitment to justice.

The late afternoon sun filtered through the blinds of the precinct's briefing room, casting long shadows across the faces of Detective Ian Mercer and Detective Sarah Langley as they prepared for another update meeting. The room was slowly filling with the rest of their team, each member carrying the weight of the long days past and the uncertainty of what was yet to come.

As they waited for everyone to settle, Ian glanced around the room, noting the tired but determined eyes of his colleagues. This case had stretched their capabilities and their endurance, but it had also pulled them into a tighter, more cohesive unit.

Sarah, sensing the collective fatigue, decided to open the meeting with a few words of encouragement. "Before we start, I just want to say—great work, everyone. These have been some of the toughest weeks we've ever faced, but I'm proud of how we've all handled it. We're not just colleagues; we're a team, and more importantly, we're friends."

Nods and murmurs of agreement echoed around the room, a small but significant lifting of spirits in the face of ongoing challenges.

Ian took over, his tone serious but infused with a warm undercurrent. "We've all made personal sacrifices to get us to this point. I know it hasn't been easy. But I also know that we couldn't have done this without each other. This kind of dedication doesn't go unnoticed, nor unappreciated."

As the briefing continued, they reviewed the latest intelligence on Wolfe's movements and discussed potential strategies. The conversation was technical and focused, yet there was an underlying sense of camaraderie that hadn't been there before, a testament to their shared experiences and mutual respect.

After the meeting, Ian and Sarah lingered in the room, gathering their notes and discussing the next steps. "You were right to acknowledge the team's effort," Ian said quietly to Sarah. "They needed that."

Sarah smiled slightly. "We all do. It's easy to get caught up in the pursuit and forget why we're doing this. Sometimes, we need to remind ourselves and each other."

They decided to take a short walk, stepping out into the crisp evening air. The precinct was quieter now, the bustling energy of the day giving way to a more reflective atmosphere.

As they walked, their conversation shifted from the case to more personal reflections. "How are you holding up, really?" Sarah asked, looking over at Ian.

Ian took a moment before answering, his gaze on the path ahead. "It's been tough. I won't lie. But having this team, having you alongside, makes it manageable. Makes me believe we can actually do this."

"And we will," Sarah affirmed, her voice steady. "We'll bring Wolfe in, and we'll see this through to the end. Together."

Their walk took them back to the precinct, ready to face whatever challenges awaited. The bonds they had strengthened over the past weeks were more than just professional necessities; they were the deep, enduring connections that would sustain them through the trials ahead.

As the chapter closed, Ian and Sarah returned to the building, their steps synchronized, a silent acknowledgment of their shared purpose and mutual trust. The precinct, with its lights glowing warmly against the encroaching darkness, was more than just a workplace; it was a testament to their dedication and unity, a beacon in the troubled night.

Chapter 16
Gathering Storm

The early morning light cast a somber glow over the precinct as Detective Ian Mercer and Detective Sarah Langley arrived, each carrying the silent weight of the impending confrontation with Adrian Wolfe. Today was the culmination of all their efforts, the final push to end a chase that had stretched their limits and tested their resolve.

In the tactical operations room, maps and screens lined the walls, displaying drone feeds and satellite imagery of the quarry where Wolfe was believed to be hiding. Officers and specialists moved about, their movements precise and purposeful, as they checked equipment and went over the plan once more.

Ian stood at the head of the briefing table, reviewing the latest intelligence reports. "Wolfe is cornered, but that makes him more dangerous," he stated, looking up at the team assembled before him. "We'll approach with caution, use drones for initial reconnaissance, and move in only when we have a clear picture of his defenses."

Sarah, who had been coordinating with the communications team, added, "All channels are secure, and backup systems are in place. We won't have a repeat of last time. We're going in with every advantage on our side."

A senior tactical advisor, Captain Moreno, detailed the approach strategy. "Two teams will flank the north and south sides of the quarry. We expect Wolfe may have traps set up, so the bomb squad will lead. No one goes in until we give the all clear."

As the team members nodded and murmured agreements, Ian continued, "Our priority is to bring Wolfe in alive. He needs to answer for what he's done, and we need to ensure that justice is served properly."

Sarah looked around the room, her expression firm yet reassuring. "This is what we've trained for. Trust your training, trust each other, and stay sharp. We all want the same outcome here—a peaceful resolution if possible."

After the briefing, Ian and Sarah stepped aside for a moment, standing by the windows overlooking the bustling city that was just beginning to wake. Ian's voice was low, tinged with the gravity of their task. "You ready for this, Sarah?"

Sarah turned to look at him, her face set with resolve. "As ready as we can be. It ends today, one way or another."

Ian nodded, his gaze turning back to the team preparing in the room. "Let's get our gear and head out. Wolfe won't wait for us."

They suited up, checking their tactical vests and communication devices. Each action was routine, yet charged with the intensity of the moment. As they prepared, other team members joined them, each carrying their own thoughts and determination into the fray.

The final checks were meticulous, with every officer ensuring their equipment was in order and their role understood. The atmosphere was one of concentrated focus; words were few, but the shared commitment was palpable.

As they loaded into the armored vehicles, the dawn light began to brighten, casting long shadows across the precinct's parking lot. The convoy was silent but for the low rumble of engines and the occasional crackle of radio checks.

The chapter closed not with a declaration of war, but with a silent, collective breath as the convoy rolled out, heading towards the quarry. Each member of the team was aware of the dangers ahead, yet driven by the duty they had sworn to uphold. The final battle with Wolfe was at hand, and each was prepared to do whatever it took to see it through to its conclusion.

Back at the precinct, while the tactical teams prepared for the physical confrontation with Adrian Wolfe, another battle was unfolding in the conference room—a battle of legal wits and maneuvers. This room, lined with law books and filled with the steady hum of conversation, was where the prosecutors and legal advisors were preparing for the aftermath of Wolfe's capture.

Assistant District Attorney Helen Briggs was at the center of the discussions, her laptop open to a complex diagram of Wolfe's known criminal activities and the potential charges he could face. Around her, a team of legal experts and police liaisons deliberated on the best strategies to ensure a watertight prosecution.

"We need to be absolutely certain that every piece of evidence we submit has an unbroken chain of custody," Helen stated firmly, addressing the room. "Wolfe is notorious for exploiting any procedural errors. We can't give him that chance."

Detective Sarah Langley, who had briefly returned from the preparations to discuss the legal aspects, added, "We've documented everything from the ground up. Every item has been logged, and we've double-checked the warrants for today's operation."

Another legal advisor, Mark Fredericks, chimed in, pointing at the screen displaying various surveillance reports. "What about the evidence we gathered under surveillance authorization? There's a chance Wolfe's defense will challenge it as invasive."

Helen nodded, her eyes scanning the documents. "We anticipated that. The surveillance was authorized under national security provisions given Wolfe's suspected ties to larger, more sinister plots. It's all been approved by a judge. Make sure that's clear in our brief."

Sarah leaned forward, her expression serious. "We should also prepare for Wolfe to try and turn the public opinion in his favor. He's manipulated media before."

"Yes, we have a PR team ready to handle the narrative," Helen confirmed. "But our focus is ensuring the legal groundwork is impeccable."

Detective Ian Mercer, who had joined the meeting after checking on the team's deployment, brought up another point. "Wolfe might also try to bargain with information. He's hinted before that he has dirt on high-profile individuals."

Helen considered this for a moment. "If he offers to cooperate, we'll need to vet the information thoroughly before making any deals. Any agreement has to provide substantial value to the public interest, not just his desire to reduce his sentence."

The conversation then shifted to the international implications of Wolfe's operations. "We've got Interpol on standby," a liaison officer reported. "Wolfe's activities crossed borders, and we'll need to coordinate with our international counterparts for some of the charges."

As the meeting drew to a close, Helen summarized their strategy. "Stay vigilant and stick to the protocol. Wolfe is cunning and desperate, but we are prepared. Let's ensure this case is as airtight as possible."

Sarah and Ian nodded, their expressions a mix of determination and the weight of the responsibility they carried. They left the conference room to rejoin the tactical teams, knowing the legal team was doing everything possible to support the day's critical operation.

The chapter closed with the legal team continuing their discussions, refining each argument and counterargument, ready to back up the actions of the tactical teams with robust legal strategies. The storm was indeed gathering, not just in the physical realm but in the courts of law where Wolfe's fate would ultimately be decided.

As the operation to capture Adrian Wolfe unfolded, the precinct's media liaison office became the epicenter of a different kind of storm. Reporters from every major news outlet had gathered, their cameras and microphones poised to capture any updates. The public's interest in the case had reached a fever pitch, driven by Wolfe's notorious reputation and the dramatic nature of his previous escape.

Inside the precinct, Detective Sarah Langley and Media Liaison Officer Greg Matthews stood facing a wall of screens, each showing different news channels broadcasting live footage from near the quarry. Greg was fielding calls on two phones, coordinating with the department's public relations team to manage the narrative.

"We need to issue a statement soon, Sarah. The speculation is rampant, and if we don't control the story, Wolfe might do it for us from wherever he's hiding," Greg said, his voice tense.

Sarah, watching the live feeds with a critical eye, nodded. "Let's reassure the public that we have the situation under control and that their safety is our top priority. We can't give out operational details, but we need to be transparent about our intentions."

Greg drafted a statement, reading it aloud to Sarah for approval: "In cooperation with federal agencies, the city police are currently engaged in a law enforcement operation aimed at apprehending a dangerous fugitive. We are taking every precaution to ensure the safety of the public and our officers. More information will be provided as it becomes available."

"Make it clear we're working with federal agencies. It adds weight to our efforts and reassures the public that this isn't just a local endeavor," Sarah suggested, her gaze still fixed on the screens.

Greg nodded, making the adjustment, then paused as another call came in. After a brief conversation, he turned to Sarah with an update. "The mayor's office is getting pressure to make a statement. They want to know if they should be preparing for any fallout."

"Tell them we're handling things on our end, and we'll brief them personally after the operation. It's crucial they don't say anything that might compromise our position or give Wolfe any advantages," Sarah responded, her tone leaving no room for argument.

As Greg relayed the message, the scene outside the precinct began to shift; more news vans arrived, and a small crowd of onlookers gathered, kept at a safe distance by police barricades. The public's anxiety was palpable, a tangible buzz that filled the air and fed the growing media frenzy.

Turning to another officer in the room, Sarah instructed, "Keep an eye on social media as well. We need to know immediately if Wolfe or anyone associated with him tries to communicate or stir up public sentiment."

"Yes, Detective," the officer replied, turning to his computer to scan various social media platforms for any signs of activity related to Wolfe.

The chapter closed with Sarah stepping outside briefly, her presence a calm authority amidst the chaos. She addressed a few questions from the press, sticking closely to the prepared statement, her words measured and reassuring. As she spoke, the cameras rolled, capturing her confident demeanor, a stark contrast to the turmoil swirling around the ongoing manhunt.

This moment encapsulated the dual challenges facing the police: capturing a dangerous fugitive while managing a restless public and a voracious media landscape, each aspect as crucial as the other in the complex tapestry of modern law enforcement.

As the sun began its descent, casting long shadows across the city, the team gathered once more in the precinct's briefing room. The mood was somber yet determined, each member acutely aware of the stakes as they awaited the final push to apprehend Adrian Wolfe. Detective Ian Mercer and Detective Sarah Langley stood side by side, embodying the leadership that had guided their team through this arduous journey.

Ian addressed the room, his voice steady, projecting a calm that belied the tension they all felt. "This is it, everyone. We've been through a lot these past weeks. It's been tough, it's tested us all. But I've never been prouder to stand with a team than I am right now with all of you."

Sarah stepped forward, her gaze sweeping over the team, each face reflecting a mix of fatigue and resolve. "We've each other's backs today, just like we always have. Remember, no one goes it alone. We are a unit, and our strength comes from our solidarity."

A veteran officer, Sergeant Ellis, who had been with the department for over two decades, stood up, his voice adding to the collective resolve. "We've faced tough odds before, but we've never faltered. Not when we stand together. Wolfe thinks he can shake us, but he's wrong. Let's bring him in and close this chapter."

Nods and murmurs of agreement filled the room, the sense of unity palpable. As the meeting concluded, team members began checking their gear, ensuring everything was in order for what could be the final confrontation.

Ian pulled Sarah aside as the room cleared. "No matter what happens out there, I want you to know—you've been the backbone of this operation. I couldn't have asked for a better partner."

Sarah smiled, a moment of warmth in the midst of pressure. "The feeling is mutual, Ian. Let's finish this the way we started—side by side."

They joined the others, who were loading into the vehicles. The convoy was silent, a collective breath held as they moved out, the city lights blurring past as they headed toward the quarry.

As they approached the staging area, Ian's radio crackled to life. "All units in position," came the voice of Captain Moreno from the tactical command vehicle.

"Copy that," Ian responded, his hand gripping the radio. Turning to his team, he reiterated, "Remember, eyes open, stay sharp, and watch out for each other. We're ending this tonight."

Sarah, checking her vest and radio, added, "Wolfe is desperate, but he's not thinking clearly anymore. That's an advantage we have. Let's use it."

The vehicles came to a stop, and the team disembarked with precision, moving into formation as they had rehearsed countless times. The quarry loomed ahead, its cavernous openings and shadows forming a daunting backdrop as the sun set behind it.

The chapter closed not with words but with action, as Ian, Sarah, and their team advanced slowly towards the quarry. Their movements were methodical, a dance of shadows against the fading light, their resolve a silent vow to protect the city and each other. The solidarity of the team, forged in the long days and nights of pursuit, was their greatest strength as they moved together into the gathering storm.

Chapter 17
The Final Plan

Under the stark lights of the mobile command unit parked a safe distance from the quarry, Detective Ian Mercer, Detective Sarah Langley, and the tactical team made their final preparations for the looming confrontation with Adrian Wolfe. The command unit was abuzz with activity; maps were spread out, screens displayed drone feeds, and officers communicated quietly but with an undercurrent of urgency.

Ian stood before the assembled team, pointing at the digital map displayed on the screen. "This is where we believe Wolfe is holed up," he indicated a dense, wooded area on the north side of the quarry. "The terrain is tricky, lots of natural cover, which he'll use to his advantage."

Sarah chimed in, holding a tablet that controlled the drone overhead. "We've got eyes in the sky, scanning for heat signatures or any unusual activity. Anything you see, report immediately."

Captain Moreno, head of the SWAT team, adjusted his tactical vest as he reviewed the positions of his team on another screen. "My team is ready to move on your command. We'll approach from two sides to box him in. The idea is to squeeze slowly, force him into a position where he has to surrender."

Ian nodded approvingly. "Exactly. We need to be methodical about this. No rash moves. Wolfe is desperate, but he's also dangerous."

One of the younger officers, Officer Jenkins, looked up from his equipment check. "Are we considering the possibility of Wolfe having explosives or other traps set up? He's been one step ahead before."

Sarah responded quickly, "Absolutely, Jenkins. That's why the bomb squad will lead. We'll clear the path before advancing. Safety is our priority."

Ian continued, "Once we have Wolfe cornered, Sarah and I will try to talk him down. Our goal is to end this peacefully if at all possible."

Another team member, Sergeant Ellis, checked his radio before speaking. "Communication lines are secure, and all frequencies are being monitored. We won't have a repeat of last time with the communications breakdown."

As the final checks were conducted, Ian's radio crackled. "Mercer, we've got movement in sector three. Could be Wolfe, or one of his men."

Ian glanced at Sarah, then back at the team. "All right, that's our cue. Positions, everyone. Let's move out with caution. Remember, watch each other's backs."

Sarah, her expression focused and determined, added, "This ends tonight. Let's bring him in and close this chapter. We owe it to the city and to ourselves."

The team acknowledged with nods and murmurs of agreement, each member checking their gear one last time before setting out. The atmosphere was charged with a mix of tension and readiness, the culmination of months of pursuit finally at hand.

As they left the command unit, the chapter closed with the team dispersing into the night, moving towards their designated positions around the quarry. The night was quiet, but the silence was deceptive, masking the strategic orchestration of the law enforcement personnel as they positioned themselves to end the long and arduous hunt for Adrian Wolfe.

The night air was thick with tension as Detective Ian Mercer and Detective Sarah Langley, along with the tactical units, moved through the dense foliage surrounding the quarry. Each member of the team knew their role, moving with precision under the cloak of darkness. The quiet was punctuated only by the soft murmurs of radio communication and the distant hum of a drone overhead.

Ian led one of the teams towards the north side of the quarry while maintaining constant communication with Sarah and the other units. Their approach was slow and methodical, designed to prevent any sudden encounters with traps that Adrian Wolfe might have set. The bomb squad, equipped with the latest technology, scanned the path ahead for any signs of explosives or other hazards.

As they advanced, Sarah coordinated with the legal team back at the precinct via her earpiece. "Confirming that all operational actions are within the legal parameters set for this engagement," she communicated, ensuring that every step they took was backed by lawful authority and that any evidence gathered during the operation would stand up in court.

The legal team, stationed in a makeshift war room filled with legal texts and monitors, kept meticulous records of the operation. Assistant District Attorney Helen Briggs oversaw this process, ready to counter any claims or challenges that might arise during or after the capture of Wolfe.

"Every move is being logged," Helen responded over the line. "We're documenting the time, location, and nature of each action for the operation's legal integrity."

Back at the quarry, Ian paused as one of the officers signaled a halt. The officer, equipped with night-vision goggles, gestured towards a suspicious area ahead. The team carefully inspected the site, finding and disabling a series of small, concealed devices that could have been used to trigger an alarm or worse. The bomb squad moved forward to disarm the devices safely, ensuring the path was clear for further advance.

With the immediate threat neutralized, Ian gave the signal to proceed. The teams resumed their cautious movement toward the quarry, aware that each step brought them closer to Wolfe.

In the shadows, Wolfe, ever cunning and resourceful, watched from a hidden vantage point. His mind raced through potential escape routes and countermeasures, but the tightening perimeter of law enforcement left him with dwindling options. The encircling presence of the tactical teams, their disciplined approach, and the comprehensive coverage from surveillance technology cut off each potential escape path he considered.

As the tactical teams converged on Wolfe's last known location, Ian and Sarah prepared for the final confrontation. They approached with the bomb squad leading, ensuring that Wolfe had no opportunity to use the environment against them.

The chapter closed with Ian and Sarah stepping cautiously into a clearing within the quarry, the drone overhead providing a live feed to the command unit and the legal team. The lights from their tactical vests pierced the darkness, illuminating the rugged terrain of the quarry. They were steps away from Wolfe's hideout, every action they took orchestrated with precision, backed by the full weight of the law and the collective resolve of their unit. The final confrontation was imminent, and they were ready to end the chase, once and for all.

As Detective Ian Mercer and Detective Sarah Langley advanced into the quarry's heart, the terrain became increasingly treacherous. The rocky ground was littered with loose stones and deep shadows cast by the moonlight, creating natural hazards that were as much a threat as the traps Adrian Wolfe might have left behind.

"Watch your step," Ian murmured to Sarah and the team following closely behind. "This area hasn't been fully cleared by the bomb squad yet."

Sarah, scanning the area with her flashlight, replied, "Let's keep the pace slow. Better to be cautious than rush into a trap."

As they moved forward, the lead bomb squad technician, Officer Daniels, held up a hand, signaling the team to stop. "Hold up," he called out softly. "We've got something here."

The team gathered around a suspicious-looking pile of debris. Officer Daniels, equipped with protective gear, carefully inspected the setup. "It's a makeshift explosive device. Looks like Wolfe wasn't planning on going quietly."

Ian looked over to Sarah, concern etching his features. "Can you disarm it?"

"We're on it," Daniels assured, his focus unwavering as he worked on the device. After a tense few minutes, he finally stepped back, nodding. "It's safe now. But keep your eyes peeled; there could be more."

Resuming their advance, the team was keenly aware that each step could spring new dangers. Their progress was slow, methodically checking every shadow and potential hiding spot for more traps.

The challenges didn't stop with physical obstacles. Ian's radio crackled to life, the voice of Captain Moreno sounding through with urgency. "Mercer, we've got a problem. One of Wolfe's associates has been spotted near the east perimeter. Looks like he might be trying to create a diversion or even aid in an escape."

Ian pressed the radio button, responding quickly. "Understood, Captain. Keep your team on him. Don't let him out of your sight. Langley and I are closing in on Wolfe."

Sarah, who had been quietly coordinating with other units, added, "I've alerted all teams to tighten the perimeter. No one gets in or out without our say."

As they approached a narrow passageway between two large boulders, a sudden noise ahead startled them. Ian signaled for quiet, and they all paused, listening. The sound of small rocks tumbling down from the boulder's side suggested movement.

Sarah whispered, "Could be Wolfe trying to slip away. Let's go."

With Ian leading, they cautiously navigated through the passageway. As they emerged on the other side, they were met with an unexpected sight—a steep drop-off that hadn't been visible on any of their maps. The quarry's edge was dangerously close, and it was clear that any wrong step could be fatal.

"Damn, this isn't on the satellite images," Ian said, peering over the edge. "Must have been a recent collapse."

Sarah checked her GPS, then shared a look with Ian. "This changes things. We need to backtrack and find another route. This area's too risky, especially in the dark."

As they turned to head back, Sarah's radio beeped. It was Helen Briggs from the legal team. "Langley, how are things progressing? We need to ensure that all actions are documented, especially with these new developments."

Sarah responded while retracing her steps, "We're adapting to the terrain and unforeseen obstacles. Everything's being recorded, Helen. We're keeping it by the book."

The chapter closed with Ian and Sarah, along with their team, carefully navigating back through the quarry to find a safer path. Each member was hyper-aware of the environment, the weight of their responsibility, and the legal implications of their actions. The night was far from over, and as they moved, the quarry seemed to echo with the challenges yet to come.

After navigating the treacherous terrain of the quarry and with the imminent capture of Adrian Wolfe, Detectives Ian Mercer and Sarah Langley found themselves momentarily back at the command vehicle, utilizing the brief respite to prepare for the next phase of their mission—the legal confrontation.

Seated in the dim light of the vehicle, maps and screens surrounding them, Ian and Sarah reviewed the extensive documentation of their operation, ensuring every detail was meticulously recorded. Sarah, her eyes scanning through digital files, spoke up, "We've got everything documented, Ian. From our entry points to the engagement protocols, and all interactions with Wolfe. It's going to be crucial for the prosecution."

Ian, looking over a printed map with annotations, nodded. "Yes, and we need to be prepared for Wolfe to use every trick in the book to challenge the legality of his capture. Helen and her team will have their work cut out for them in court."

Just then, Assistant District Attorney Helen Briggs joined them via a video call on the laptop set up on a makeshift table. Her expression was serious but confident. "Ian, Sarah, I've been going over the evidence and your field reports. We have a strong case, but Wolfe will undoubtedly focus on any potential procedural missteps. We need to be watertight on every detail."

Sarah responded, "We're clear on our side, Helen. The operation was conducted within the full bounds of the law. Wolfe's rights were respected throughout, despite his lack of cooperation."

Helen's face softened slightly, "I know you both did everything by the book. That's why it's important we present a united front. The defense will try to exploit any perceived division between the operational and legal aspects of this case."

Ian leaned closer to the laptop, his tone firm. "There's no division here, Helen. We all want the same thing—to see Wolfe answer for his crimes in a court of law."

Helen nodded, "Exactly. And remember, the public will be watching closely. The way we handle this case could set precedents for future operations. We're not just trying Wolfe; we're potentially shaping policy."

Sarah took a deep breath, reflecting on the magnitude of their undertaking. "It's more than just a trial, isn't it? It's about proving that the system works, that it can handle even the most challenging and manipulative criminals like Wolfe."

"Yes," Helen agreed, "and it's about restoring public trust. The community needs to see that justice is not only done but done fairly and transparently."

Ian looked at Sarah, then back at Helen. "We'll be ready. After everything we've been through, we owe it to ourselves and the city to bring this to a proper closure."

As the call ended, Ian and Sarah gathered the final reports and digital recordings, placing them into a secure case. They then stepped out of the vehicle, joining the rest of their team who were preparing to transport Wolfe to the detention center.

The chapter closed with Ian and Sarah watching as Wolfe was led away in handcuffs, surrounded by officers. They did not speak, but their shared glance spoke volumes—of relief, of tired satisfaction, and of steeling themselves for the battles yet to come, not in the streets, but in the courtroom. Their resolve was clear; this was the end of one chapter and the beginning of another critical phase of their mission.

Chapter 18
The Ultimate Sacrifice

The courtroom was hushed as the trial of Adrian Wolfe began, a trial that had captured the attention of the city and beyond. The gallery was packed, with members of the public and press crammed into every available space, their eyes fixed on the figures at the center of the room. At the defense table, Adrian Wolfe sat stoically, his gaze occasionally sweeping across the room with a calm, unnerving poise.

At the prosecution's table, Assistant District Attorney Helen Briggs was arranging her papers, her expression one of focused determination. Beside her, Detective Ian Mercer and Detective Sarah Langley sat as key witnesses, their roles crucial in the unfolding drama.

The judge, an experienced jurist known for her stern courtroom management, called the room to order. "This court is now in session. We are here to proceed with the case of the People vs. Adrian Wolfe. The charges are numerous and serious, and it is this court's duty to ensure a fair and just trial."

As the opening statements began, Helen Briggs stood, addressing the jury with a clear and resonant voice. "Ladies and gentlemen of the jury, over the course of this trial, you will hear and see evidence that Adrian Wolfe orchestrated and executed a series of criminal activities that not only broke the law but endangered the lives of countless individuals. His actions were premeditated, calculated, and harmful beyond measure."

Wolfe's defense attorney, a well-known criminal lawyer with a reputation for handling high-profile cases, countered vigorously. "While the prosecution will attempt to paint Mr. Wolfe as a mastermind of chaos, it is crucial to remember that in our justice system, the burden of proof lies with the accuser. We intend to show that Mr. Wolfe's actions, while admittedly unconventional, were not criminal as charged."

The tension in the room was palpable as witnesses were called to the stand. Forensic experts, tactical team members, and financial analysts provided testimony, each piece of evidence scrutinized under the watchful eyes of the jury and the public.

Ian and Sarah, waiting for their turns to testify, observed the proceedings with an intensity borne of months of hard work and personal sacrifice. Their testimony would be key to providing an inside view of Wolfe's operations and the dangers they posed.

During a recess, Ian leaned over to Sarah, whispering, "Once we're up there, it's all about the facts. Just lay out what we know, what we saw, and what we did."

Sarah nodded, her face set in a mask of resolve. "I know. It's just hard to sit here and listen to them trying to twist everything we worked so hard to uncover."

Ian gave her a reassuring look. "We've done our part, and we'll continue to do so. Wolfe will face justice."

As the court resumed, the atmosphere was charged with anticipation. The next few days would see a deep dive into the complex web of deceit and manipulation that Wolfe had woven around his victims and the city.

The chapter closed on the courtroom, a silent battleground of legal and moral confrontation. Wolfe, ever composed, watched the proceedings with an unreadable expression, while the prosecution and defense geared up for a rigorous examination of facts and intentions. This was more than just a trial; it was a test of the resilience and integrity of the legal system itself.

The courtroom was tense as Detective Ian Mercer took the stand, his presence commanding immediate attention. As he was sworn in, his gaze briefly met Adrian Wolfe's, a silent acknowledgment of the many chess moves between them now culminating in this critical moment.

Assistant District Attorney Helen Briggs approached the stand, her questions precise and aimed to draw a clear narrative for the jury. "Detective Mercer, can you describe the nature of the operations led by Adrian Wolfe, based on your investigation?"

Ian's voice was steady, his response meticulous. "Wolfe orchestrated a series of complex criminal activities, ranging from extortion to unlawful surveillance, and manipulation of public officials. His operations were highly structured, suggesting both a deep understanding of criminal enterprise and a disregard for the law."

The defense attorney, Mr. Reynolds, was quick to cross-examine. "Detective Mercer, isn't it true that much of the evidence collected against my client was circumstantial? How can you be sure that my client was the mastermind and not merely an associate?"

Ian responded without hesitation. "The evidence is not merely circumstantial. We intercepted communications directly involving Mr. Wolfe, detailing his instructions for various illegal activities. Furthermore, we recovered digital evidence from his secure servers, which directly implicates him in these operations."

As Ian detailed the technical aspects of the investigation, Sarah prepared for her testimony. She knew that her insights into Wolfe's psychological tactics would be crucial.

When Sarah was called to the stand, Helen's line of questioning shifted to focus on the impact of Wolfe's actions. "Detective Langley, can you speak to the effect Mr. Wolfe's actions had on the community?"

Sarah looked directly at the jury, her tone earnest. "Wolfe's actions created a state of fear and uncertainty. He manipulated individuals to the point where they doubted their own judgment, making it easier for him to control them. The psychological impact on the victims was profound, and the ripple effects were felt throughout the community."

Reynolds was quick to challenge her. "Detective Langley, isn't it true that fear and uncertainty can be subjective? How can you attribute these feelings directly to my client without considering other societal factors?"

Sarah was prepared for this. "While it's true that fear can have multiple sources, in this case, the direct correlation between Wolfe's actions and the increase in fear and uncertainty among the victims was clear. We conducted extensive interviews and psychological assessments to support this conclusion."

The courtroom drama intensified as technical experts and psychologists were also brought in to testify, each adding layers to the prosecution's case, while the defense continued to probe for any weaknesses in their arguments.

During a recess, Ian and Sarah conferred with Helen. "They're going to keep trying to poke holes in the psychological evidence," Sarah noted, concern evident in her voice.

Helen nodded, reviewing her notes. "Yes, but your testimony was strong, and the expert statements are solid. We'll keep reinforcing the direct links between Wolfe's actions and their consequences. It's about painting the full picture, making it clear that Wolfe's intent was to harm and control."

Ian added, "We just need to stay focused and clear. The truth is on our side."

As the court resumed, the atmosphere was charged with the gravity of the unfolding testimonies. Each statement, each piece of evidence, built towards a climax that would determine not only the fate of Adrian Wolfe but also the very notions of justice and accountability in the face of such calculated malevolence.

The chapter closed with the courtroom in a state of heightened anticipation, each side bracing for the next round of legal and moral combat, where every word and every piece of evidence could tip the scales of justice.

In a dramatic turn of events in the courtroom, Adrian Wolfe took the stand, his demeanor calm and collected, his gaze occasionally sweeping across the jury and courtroom spectators. His defense lawyer, Mr. Reynolds, stood by, ready to guide Wolfe through a narrative designed to sow doubt and highlight his client's alleged motivations beyond mere criminal intent.

"Mr. Wolfe, could you please explain to the court your actions and what you intended to achieve?" Reynolds began, giving Wolfe the floor to articulate his defense.

Wolfe leaned slightly forward, his voice smooth and controlled. "Certainly. While I acknowledge that my methods might have been unconventional, my aim was to expose systemic corruption and complacency in our society. I sought to challenge the status quo, to force people to question and confront the realities often ignored."

Reynolds nodded, prompting further, "And in doing so, did you ever intend to harm individuals or break the law as the prosecution claims?"

Wolfe shook his head, his expression one of sincerity. "My goal was never to harm, but to enlighten. Yes, I orchestrated scenarios that required individuals to face difficult truths, but it was always with the intention of bringing about greater awareness and change."

Assistant District Attorney Helen Briggs watched Wolfe's performance intently, prepared to dismantle his arguments during cross-examination. Meanwhile, Detectives Ian Mercer and Sarah Langley exchanged skeptical glances, aware of Wolfe's skill in manipulation.

Reynolds continued, steering the narrative towards the ethical implications of Wolfe's actions. "You've been accused of severe crimes, Mr. Wolfe. How do you reconcile your actions with the accusations laid against you?"

Wolfe paused, his eyes scanning the courtroom. "In challenging systems, one often has to operate at the edges of convention. I admit, my approach was radical, but so are the issues I sought to address. If my actions have led us to this discourse today, to this very examination of justice and society, then I believe they have served a meaningful purpose."

As Reynolds concluded his examination, Helen stood, her presence commanding as she approached Wolfe for the cross-examination. "Mr. Wolfe, you speak of enlightenment and societal change, but isn't it true that your actions led to real harm? People were manipulated, frightened, and hurt by your so-called 'experiments.'"

Wolfe's demeanor remained unfazed. "While regrettable, these reactions were sometimes necessary to jolt individuals out of complacency. Great change is seldom achieved without discomfort."

Helen pressed on, her tone sharp. "Is it not also true that you benefited financially from these 'experiments'? This wasn't just about ideology, was it, Mr. Wolfe? You profited from the fear and chaos you created."

Wolfe's composure finally seemed to crack slightly, a flicker of irritation crossing his face. "One must fund their endeavors somehow. The financial aspects were merely a means to sustain the greater mission."

As the cross-examination continued, Wolfe's manipulative eloquence began to unravel, revealing the calculated and self-serving nature of his actions. Helen expertly navigated through his defenses, highlighting inconsistencies and ulterior motives.

The chapter closed with the courtroom in a state of heightened tension. Wolfe's testimony had revealed the complexity of his character and his actions, leaving the jury and public conflicted and intrigued. His manipulation within the courtroom mirrored his manipulation outside it, leaving all to wonder just how deep his deceit could run. The battle in court was not just legal but psychological, a fight for justice against a backdrop of philosophical and moral quandaries.

The trial had reached a crucial juncture, with the tension palpable in the courtroom. After days of intense testimony and legal arguments, it was clear that the outcome would hinge not just on facts, but on the jurors' perception of Adrian Wolfe's motivations and the moral implications of his actions.

Detective Ian Mercer was called back to the stand, this time to discuss the direct impacts of Wolfe's actions on the community and law enforcement. Assistant District Attorney Helen Briggs prepared to delve into the sacrifices made during the investigation.

"Ian, can you describe for the court the extent of the sacrifices made by your team in pursuing Mr. Wolfe?" Helen asked, her voice steady.

Ian nodded, his expression solemn. "This investigation demanded extraordinary measures from everyone involved. We had officers who spent countless hours away from their families, enduring significant personal risk. We even had casualties—officers injured in the line of duty, directly as a result of Wolfe's traps and manipulations."

Helen followed up, pressing the point home. "And would you say that these sacrifices were a direct consequence of Mr. Wolfe's actions?"

"Absolutely," Ian affirmed. "Every step we took was a response to an aggressive and dangerous scheme orchestrated by Wolfe. The risks we encountered were unlike any typical criminal pursuit. Wolfe's actions were calculated to cause maximum disruption and danger."

The defense attorney, Mr. Reynolds, rose for the cross-examination, his tone skeptical. "Detective Mercer, isn't risk a part of your job? How can you attribute normal occupational hazards directly to my client?"

Ian's response was resolute. "While risk is indeed part of our job, the level and nature of the risks imposed by Mr. Wolfe were far beyond the norm. His actions were specifically designed to thwart law enforcement efforts through dangerous means. This wasn't about evading capture through typical criminal behavior; it was about creating a warzone."

As Ian stepped down, the atmosphere in the courtroom was charged. The jury seemed deeply affected by the testimony about the sacrifices made by the police. It was a poignant reminder of the human cost of Wolfe's so-called societal experiments.

The closing arguments by both sides were potent and compelling. Helen emphasized the need for justice not only for the direct victims of Wolfe's actions but also for the community and law enforcement who had suffered greatly.

Reynolds argued that Wolfe's intentions to expose societal flaws should mitigate the perception of his guilt, suggesting that his methods, while extreme, were aimed at a greater good.

As the jury retired to deliberate, the courtroom buzzed with anxious speculation. Ian and Sarah sat together, their conversation low and introspective.

Sarah whispered, "Whatever happens, we've done everything we could. We've brought the truth to light, no matter how painful."

Ian nodded, his gaze fixed on the jury room door. "Yes, we've done our part. Now it's up to them to decide what justice looks like in this case."

The chapter closed not with the jury's verdict, but with Ian and Sarah standing together, reflecting on the long road they had traveled. They had made sacrifices, faced dangers, and now, as the twilight filtered through the courthouse windows, they waited for the resolution of a case that had changed them both profoundly. Their commitment to justice had been tested, and they had met that challenge with unwavering dedication, embodying the very essence of the ultimate sacrifice.

As the courthouse began to empty, the subdued hum of conversations filling the corridor, Ian Mercer and Sarah Langley found themselves in a quiet corner, processing the intense culmination of their long and arduous journey. The jury was still out, deliberating the fate of Adrian Wolfe, but for Ian and Sarah, this moment was about more than just the verdict; it was about understanding the depth of their sacrifices and the broader implications of their pursuit of justice.

Ian leaned against the cool marble wall, his gaze reflective. "Do you ever wonder if it was all worth it? The long hours, the danger, the personal cost?"

Sarah looked at him, her eyes equally contemplative. "Every day. But then I think about the lives we've potentially saved, the corrupt schemes we've exposed... It gives me some peace, knowing that our work has meaning beyond the immediate pain."

Ian nodded slowly, "I get that. It's just—seeing everything laid out in court, hearing how our actions impacted not just Wolfe but also the community... it's heavy."

Sarah sighed, "It is. But that weight is something we chose to carry the moment we took the oath to serve and protect. Wolfe's actions forced us to confront the darker sides of our society, and our response, hopefully, reaffirms the public's trust in us."

Their conversation was momentarily interrupted as Helen Briggs approached, her expression one of cautious optimism. "The jury seems to be taking their role seriously. They're asking the right questions, according to the notes passed to the judge. It's a good sign—they understand the complexity of the case."

Ian gave a small smile, "That's reassuring to hear. Thanks, Helen."

Helen paused before adding, "You know, regardless of the outcome, the case you both built was solid. You've done everything possible to ensure justice is served. Remember that."

As Helen walked away, Sarah turned back to Ian. "Whatever happens next, we need to remember why we started this journey. Wolfe challenged the very foundations of our beliefs and practices. We had to rise to that challenge."

Ian's reply was thoughtful. "True. And in doing so, we've maybe set a precedent for how deeply law enforcement can—and should—engage with systemic issues. It's bigger than just arresting the bad guys; it's about understanding and addressing the underlying causes."

Sarah nodded, her voice firm. "Exactly. And our role in that is just beginning. This trial, whatever the verdict, is a reminder of our responsibilities. It's about more than just law enforcement; it's about being guardians of justice."

The chapter closed with Ian and Sarah looking out of the large courthouse windows, watching as the city moved below them. The streets were bustling with life, unaware of the gravity of the decisions being made above. For Ian and Sarah, the trial was a profound moment of reflection on their roles as defenders of peace and justice, a testament to their dedication and the sacrifices they had made. As they turned to rejoin their colleagues, their conversation faded into a shared, silent resolve to continue their mission, no matter what challenges lay ahead.

Chapter 19
The Aftermath

The jury's verdict was in, and the tension that had enveloped the courthouse now reached its peak. As Detective Ian Mercer and Detective Sarah Langley entered the courtroom to hear the decision, the gravity of the moment was palpable. The murmurs of the crowd ceased as everyone took their seats, their eyes fixed on the jury box where twelve individuals were about to determine Adrian Wolfe's fate.

The judge called the room to order with a stern voice that resonated through the silent courtroom. "Will the defendant please rise?" she directed.

Adrian Wolfe stood, his demeanor composed, his eyes scanning the room slowly, taking in the faces of those who had worked tirelessly to see him convicted.

The foreman of the jury stood, a piece of paper trembling slightly in his hand. "In the case of the People versus Adrian Wolfe, on the count of conspiracy to commit criminal activities, we find the defendant... guilty. On the count of endangering public safety, we find the defendant... guilty."

As each guilty verdict was announced, a subdued reaction rippled through the courtroom. Ian and Sarah exchanged a brief look—a mix of relief and somber acknowledgment of what it had taken to get to this point.

After the court was dismissed, they stepped outside, where the media had gathered, eager for comments. Sarah addressed the reporters first. "Today's verdict is not just a victory for us; it's a victory for the city. It's a message that no one is above the law, no matter how sophisticated or deep their operations may run."

Ian added, "It's also a testament to the hard work of our team who put in countless hours ensuring that justice was served. We hope that today's verdict brings some peace to those affected by Wolfe's actions."

As the crowd dispersed, Ian and Sarah walked back to their precinct, the weight of the long months leading up to the trial momentarily lifted. But the quiet of the evening brought a reflective mood.

Back at their desks, Sarah sighed, turning to Ian. "What are you thinking?"

Ian looked up, his face weary yet resolute. "Just about everything we went through. The risks, the challenges... and what it means going forward. Today was a closure, but the work doesn't end here."

Sarah nodded, her expression thoughtful. "It doesn't. There's going to be a lot of rebuilding to do. Trust to regain, policies to review. Wolfe's trial might be over, but the effects of his crimes will linger."

Ian leaned back in his chair, rubbing his temples. "Yeah, and there's the personal toll it took on all of us. We need to make sure our team gets the support they need to process this. Maybe push for more comprehensive mental health resources."

"That's a good point," Sarah agreed. "I'll bring it up with the captain tomorrow. It's crucial we don't just move on to the next case without addressing the fallout from this one."

Their conversation was interrupted by a junior detective knocking on Ian's office door. "Detective Mercer, Detective Langley, the captain wants to debrief the whole team first thing tomorrow. She's planning a review of the entire operation."

"Thanks, we'll be there," Ian responded, then turned back to Sarah once they were alone again. "Looks like the reckoning has just begun."

The chapter closed with Ian and Sarah preparing to leave the precinct. The city lights glimmered outside, a stark reminder of the world that continued to move forward. Inside, the quiet of the office was a stark contrast, reflective of the internal contemplations of two detectives who had just navigated one of their toughest cases yet. The road ahead was clear, filled with both challenges and opportunities for growth.

In the weeks following the trial, the city began a slow process of recovery and reflection. Detective Sarah Langley took the initiative to engage more actively with community leaders and citizens, participating in forums and discussions about law enforcement and community relations. Meanwhile, Detective Ian Mercer focused on internal department reforms, working closely with the police academy to enhance training programs that emphasized ethical policing and community engagement.

One bright Saturday, a community event was organized in a local park, aimed at fostering a better relationship between the police and the community. Booths were set up, offering information on personal safety, legal rights, and police procedures. Activities for children were scattered throughout, and local food vendors provided a festive atmosphere.

Sarah, standing next to a booth set up by the police department, handed out pamphlets and chatted with residents. "We're here to answer any questions you might have about the police work and how we can better serve you," she explained to a curious group of locals.

A local community leader, Mrs. Thompson, approached her, a smile of appreciation on her face. "Detective Langley, it's good to see the department reaching out like this. After everything that's happened, it's going to take time to rebuild trust, but this is a good start."

Sarah nodded, acknowledging the long road ahead. "Thank you, Mrs. Thompson. We understand there's a lot to be done, and we're committed to making real changes. It's about more than just responding to crime; it's about being a part of the community."

Elsewhere in the park, Ian observed the interactions between his officers and the community, noting the relaxed conversations and the laughter of children as they climbed into a police car on display. He was approached by a reporter from the local newspaper, who was covering the event.

"Detective Mercer, can you tell us how the police department plans to maintain this momentum of community engagement?" the reporter asked, her recorder in hand.

Ian thought for a moment before answering. "We're integrating community interaction into our regular operations, not just as an occasional event. We want the officers to know the areas they patrol on a deeper level, understand the people, and be seen as a helping hand, not just enforcers."

The event continued with a brief ceremony where the police department recognized several community members for their roles in aiding the investigation and maintaining peace during the trying times of Adrian Wolfe's capture and trial. Sarah and Ian both gave short speeches about the importance of community support in their work.

As the day wound down, the crowd began to disperse, leaving Sarah and Ian to reflect on the event's success. "It feels like we're turning a page, doesn't it?" Ian remarked, watching a family walk away with balloons and a football they had won in a raffle.

Sarah smiled, her eyes following the same family. "It does. Today was about showing that we're here for them, not just when there's trouble but all the time. It's these small steps that will help heal the wounds."

The chapter closed with the park slowly emptying, the remnants of the day's activities being packed away. In the quiet that followed, Ian and Sarah shared a moment of contemplative silence, both aware of the challenges still to come but reassured by the community's response. They were ready to face the future, armed with the lessons learned and the relationships built during this pivotal time.

Late one evening, after a long day filled with meetings and planning sessions for the department's ongoing reforms, Ian Mercer found himself alone in his office, staring out at the city skyline. The quiet of the night provided a stark contrast to the constant buzz of activity that had defined his days recently. The solitude prompted a rare moment of introspection for Ian, a chance to contemplate his journey through the complex case of Adrian Wolfe.

As he sat in the dim light, his longtime partner, Detective Sarah Langley, knocked softly and entered, her presence a comforting reminder of the shared experiences that had bonded them deeply.

"Hey, you're still here. Burning the midnight oil?" Sarah asked, taking a seat across from him.

Ian half-smiled, turning away from the window. "Yeah, just thinking about everything. This case... it's changed me, Sarah."

Sarah nodded, understanding the sentiment. "It's been a tough road. But you've handled it with incredible integrity, Ian. I've seen you make decisions that weren't just about solving a case, but about doing what's right."

Ian sighed, leaning back in his chair. "I've been thinking about that. About what 'right' really means in our line of work. Wolfe challenged us, pushed us to our limits. I keep wondering if there was something we could have done differently."

"You mean in how we handled Wolfe?" Sarah asked, her tone gentle yet probing.

"Yes, exactly. Did we push too hard? Did we miss signs that could have led to a different outcome?" Ian's voice was tinged with doubt, a rare admission of his inner uncertainties.

Sarah leaned forward, her eyes earnest. "Ian, we did our jobs. We protected the public and upheld the law. Wolfe was a catalyst for a lot of things, but we can't take responsibility for his actions. We responded to the situation as best we could with the information we had."

Ian nodded slowly, taking in her words. "I know you're right. It's just hard not to replay it all, wondering about the what-ifs."

"That's because you care," Sarah said softly. "It's what makes you a good detective, Ian. But at some point, we have to accept that we've done everything within our power and responsibility. The rest isn't ours to carry."

Ian was quiet for a moment, then looked at Sarah with a rueful smile. "What would I do without you, Sarah?"

Sarah smiled back, her presence reassuring. "Probably stay here all night staring at the skyline. Come on, let's get some dinner. You need a break."

As they stood and gathered their things, Ian's gaze lingered on the city one more time. "You're right. Let's go."

The chapter closed with Ian and Sarah leaving the precinct together, the weight of the past weeks still lingering but tempered by the solid foundation of their partnership and friendship. As they stepped out into the cool night air, Ian felt a measure of peace, a recognition that while the work was never truly done, they had navigated their latest challenge with dedication and had emerged ready to face whatever came next.

After dinner, Ian Mercer and Sarah Langley decided to take a slow walk through the city park, a place far removed from the turmoil of their professional lives. The park was quiet at this hour, with only a few distant sounds of traffic and the occasional rustle of leaves in the gentle night breeze. The serenity of the environment offered a stark contrast to the high-stress atmosphere of the precinct.

Sarah broke the comfortable silence between them. "You know, Ian, it's evenings like these that remind me why we do what we do. It's not just about catching the bad guys. It's about making sure there's a safe place for moments like this."

Ian smiled, appreciating the sentiment. "Absolutely. It's easy to forget that when you're caught up in the chaos of a case like Wolfe's. You've been incredible through all of this, Sarah. I couldn't have asked for a better partner."

Sarah glanced at him, a playful smirk crossing her lips. "Are you getting sentimental in your old age, Mercer?"

Ian chuckled. "Maybe just a bit. But seriously, I mean it. We've been through a lot together, and this case... it really brought home how much I rely on you, not just professionally but personally."

Sarah nodded, her expression softening. "I feel the same, Ian. We've supported each other through some tough times. It's more than just partnership at this point. It's a deep bond, a real friendship."

They continued walking, their steps in sync. "Do you ever think about what comes next?" Ian asked after a moment. "I mean, after all this—after our careers, what's the end game?"

Sarah considered the question. "I think about it sometimes. I hope to leave a legacy of integrity and courage, something that will inspire the new officers, maybe even change the department for the better. What about you?"

"I think much the same," Ian replied. "I'd like to think that when I'm done, I've made a real difference, maybe trained up the next generation of detectives who can carry on the work with the same dedication."

They reached a bench overlooking a small, illuminated fountain and sat down. The sound of the water was calming, a natural backdrop to their contemplative mood.

Sarah turned to Ian. "We've still got a good run left in us, though. There are more cases, more challenges. And I can't imagine facing them with anyone but you."

Ian looked at her, a genuine smile playing across his face. "Here's to facing whatever comes next, together."

They sat in silence for a few more moments, each lost in their thoughts but comforted by the presence of the other. Finally, Sarah stood up, stretching slightly. "We should probably head back. It's getting late, and we have another long day tomorrow."

As they walked back to their cars, the connection between them was palpable, strengthened not just by the trials they had faced but by the mutual respect and understanding that had grown between them over the years. They knew whatever challenges awaited them in the future, they would face them together, their bond a solid foundation that would support them both personally and professionally.

The chapter closed as they said their goodnights, the city lights casting long shadows on their path. It was a scene of quiet strength and partnership, a fitting reflection of their journey and the deeper connection they had forged in the crucible of their work.

Chapter 20
A New Dawn

In the wake of the high-profile case against Adrian Wolfe, the city was poised on the brink of significant change. The police department faced scrutiny and the prospect of reforms, a process initiated by the internal inquiry into the conduct of the operation that had brought Wolfe to justice. This inquiry, thorough and at times painfully meticulous, was nearing its conclusion.

The precinct conference room was silent as the final meeting to discuss the findings of the inquiry took place. Senior officers, along with key members of the city council and representatives from the mayor's office, gathered around the large oak table that dominated the room. Files and digital devices were neatly arranged in front of each participant, the air heavy with anticipation.

Detective Ian Mercer and Detective Sarah Langley, central figures in the Wolfe case, were present, their roles as witnesses and contributors to the inquiry now giving way to observers of its outcome. The head of the inquiry, a seasoned internal affairs officer named Captain Helena Ford, stood at the head of the table, clearing her throat before she began to speak.

"Ladies and gentlemen, over the past several months, we have conducted a comprehensive review of the actions taken during the operation that led to the arrest of Adrian Wolfe," Captain Ford began, her voice steady and authoritative. "This review included interviews with involved officers, analysis of tactical decisions, and evaluations of procedural adherence."

She paused to allow her words to sink in before continuing, "Our findings conclude that while there were minor procedural oversights, these did not compromise the integrity of the operation or the safety of the public. The primary actors, including Detectives Mercer and Langley, performed their duties with commendable dedication and within the bounds of the law."

A subtle sigh of relief was palpable among some of the attendees, particularly Ian and Sarah, whose careers and reputations had rested heavily on the outcome of this inquiry.

Captain Ford addressed the room again, "However, the inquiry has also highlighted areas where improvements are necessary. These include the integration of new technologies for surveillance and evidence collection, enhanced training programs focusing on ethical decision-making, and increased transparency in our operations with the public."

The room listened intently as Captain Ford outlined the recommendations for reform, which were comprehensive and aimed at not just correcting past inadequacies but also preparing the department for future challenges.

"As part of these reforms, we will be initiating community outreach programs to build stronger relationships with the citizens we serve," Captain Ford concluded, her gaze sweeping across the room to gauge reactions.

The meeting moved into a more interactive phase, with city council members asking questions and discussing the implications of the reforms. The tone was constructive, with a clear recognition of the need for change balanced by an appreciation of the challenges faced by law enforcement.

Ian and Sarah, while mostly silent during this phase, exchanged looks that conveyed their approval of the direction the discussions were taking. They understood that their actions during the Wolfe case had set these changes in motion, and both felt a profound sense of responsibility to contribute positively to the reform process going forward.

As the meeting drew to a close, the mood was cautiously optimistic. There was a sense that while the road ahead would be demanding, the foundation laid by the inquiry's findings and recommendations would guide the department toward a more effective and community-oriented approach.

The chapter closed with the room slowly emptying, the participants deep in thought or in quiet conversation as they left. Ian and Sarah remained seated for a moment longer, reflecting on the journey that had brought them here and the new dawn that the resolution of the inquiry promised for their city and their careers. The challenges of the past were now stepping stones to a future that they were ready to shape.

In the weeks following the resolution of the inquiry, Detective Sarah Langley took the lead in a series of community restoration initiatives. These efforts were designed not only to heal the wounds left by the recent turmoil but also to foster a deeper, more resilient bond between the police force and the community it served.

At a community center located in one of the neighborhoods most affected by the crimes linked to Adrian Wolfe, Sarah stood before a diverse audience of local residents, business owners, and young people. Next to her was Detective Ian Mercer, along with community leaders and other officers involved in the outreach programs.

Sarah addressed the gathering, her voice resonant and clear. "Thank you all for coming today. It's essential that we come together to discuss how we can move forward as a community. The recent events have tested us all, but they've also shown us the strength we have when we work together."

A local business owner raised his hand, his expression one of cautious optimism. "Detective Langley, we appreciate what you're doing. What specific steps are being planned to ensure that what happened with Wolfe doesn't happen again?"

Sarah nodded, expecting this question. "We are implementing several key changes. First, we're enhancing our community policing efforts. This means you'll see officers more frequently, not just on patrol, but participating in community events, getting to know you and your concerns."

Ian added, "We're also upgrading our training programs to focus more on ethics and community relations. It's important that every officer understands that their role is not just to enforce the law but to serve as guardians of the community's welfare."

Another resident, a mother of two young children, chimed in. "What about the youth? How can we ensure our kids feel safe and supported?"

Sarah smiled, glad to address this. "Great question. We're launching mentorship programs where officers will work directly with young people, offering guidance and support. We want our youth to see officers as role models and allies."

A teenager in the audience, who had been listening intently, spoke up. "Will there be opportunities for us to tell you what we need? Sometimes it feels like decisions are made without our input."

Ian responded, his tone encouraging. "Absolutely. Part of our new initiative is to hold regular forums just like this one where everyone, especially our young people, can voice their needs and concerns. We're here to listen and act on what you tell us."

The community leader, Mrs. Thompson, stood up, her voice strong and full of conviction. "I want to thank Detectives Langley and Mercer for their honesty and commitment. It's going to be a long road, but having open conversations like this, where we can express our concerns and hear directly from you, makes me hopeful about our future."

Sarah concluded the meeting with a promise. "We're committed to this journey with you. Today is just the beginning. Let's keep this dialogue open, and together, we'll build a community where everyone feels safe and valued."

As the meeting adjourned, people gathered in small groups, continuing their conversations. The atmosphere was cautiously positive, with many expressing relief and renewed hope.

Ian and Sarah stepped aside, allowing the community members to interact with the other officers. Watching the interactions, Ian remarked quietly to Sarah, "It feels like we're finally making real progress."

Sarah nodded, watching a young officer laugh with a group of teenagers. "It does. It's about change, Ian. Real change that lasts."

The chapter closed on the community center, now buzzing with discussion and laughter. Outside, the setting sun cast a warm glow over the scene, symbolizing the new dawn that was slowly rising over the community, promising brighter days ahead driven by mutual respect and understanding.

The evening found Detective Ian Mercer alone in his favorite spot by the riverside, a secluded area where the city seemed distant, and the water's gentle flow provided a soothing backdrop. It was here that Ian often came to think, especially when the weight of his badge seemed heaviest.

As he watched the sun dip below the horizon, painting the sky in shades of orange and purple, his thoughts wandered through the events of the past months—the challenges, the victories, and the losses. The solitude allowed him a rare opportunity to introspect on his personal journey through the tumultuous case of Adrian Wolfe.

Lost in thought, Ian didn't notice Sarah approaching until she was almost beside him. "Mind if I join you?" she asked, her voice soft in the quiet of the evening.

"Not at all," Ian replied, managing a smile as he patted the bench next to him. "Just doing some thinking."

Sarah sat down, following his gaze out over the water. "It's a good spot for it. What's on your mind?"

Ian sighed, the words coming slowly. "Just reflecting on everything that's happened. Wolfe's case pushed me in ways I hadn't expected. Made me question a lot about what we do and why we do it."

Sarah nodded, understanding. "It's been a rough ride. But you handled it with incredible strength, Ian. You've grown a lot through this whole process."

"Have I?" Ian turned to her, genuinely curious. "Sometimes I wonder. There were moments I felt I was barely holding on."

"That's just it, though," Sarah said gently. "Growth isn't about never struggling. It's about pushing through those struggles, learning from them. You did more than just hold on, Ian. You led us through one of the toughest cases we've ever faced. And you made decisions that not only resolved the case but honored the integrity of our badge."

Ian considered her words, letting them sink in. "I guess when you put it like that, it does feel like growth. It's just hard to see when you're in the middle of it all."

"That's why we have partners," Sarah smiled, giving him a light nudge. "To help us see the things we might miss on our own."

Ian chuckled, the sound mingling with the rustle of leaves in the breeze. "I don't know what I would have done without you, Sarah. You've been more than a partner through all of this."

"And you've been more than a partner to me, too," Sarah replied sincerely. "We've both come out of this changed, I think. Stronger, hopefully."

The conversation paused as both detectives sat quietly, each lost in their thoughts but comforted by the presence of the other. Finally, Ian spoke again. "You know, I think I'm ready for whatever comes next. Wolfe's case closed a chapter for me, but it's opened another. One where I feel more prepared, more... aware of what I'm capable of."

"That's the spirit," Sarah agreed. "And whatever comes next, we'll face it together. Like we always do."

The chapter closed with Ian and Sarah sitting in silence, watching as the last light of the day faded into the soft glow of twilight. The challenges they had faced had indeed been formidable, but they had emerged not just unscathed but enriched by the experience, ready to meet the future with renewed purpose and undeniable resolve. Their partnership, strengthened by adversity, promised to be their greatest asset as they continued to serve and protect in a world that was ever-changing.

The dawn of a new day brought a symbolic fresh start for Detectives Ian Mercer and Sarah Langley. As they walked into the precinct, the energy was noticeably different. There was a sense of renewal that permeated the air, fueled by the department's recent shifts in policy and the successful integration of the community outreach programs they had championed.

In the precinct's main hall, Captain Helena Ford had gathered the team for an announcement, her demeanor upbeat as she addressed her officers. "Good morning, everyone. As you all are aware, we've been through some significant changes recently. Today, I'm pleased to introduce the launch of our new community liaison unit, which will be a bridge between our officers and the neighborhoods we serve."

Ian and Sarah exchanged smiles, their project coming to fruition. After the captain's speech, Ian turned to Sarah. "It feels like we're finally seeing the results of all that hard work."

Sarah nodded, her eyes reflecting a mix of pride and anticipation. "It's just the beginning, but it's a good start. It's going to make a real difference, Ian. I believe that."

The captain called them over, her expression serious yet kind. "Mercer, Langley, I want you both to help lead this new unit. Your experience and your approach to community engagement during the Wolfe case were exemplary. You understand what it takes to build trust and maintain safety."

Ian was taken aback, a slight flush of pride coloring his cheeks. "Thank you, Captain. We'd be honored. Right, Sarah?"

"Absolutely," Sarah affirmed, her enthusiasm evident. "This is exactly the kind of work we've been hoping to push forward."

As the meeting dispersed, Ian and Sarah discussed their plans for the new unit. "We need to set some solid goals for the first few months," Ian suggested as they headed to their new office, a space dedicated to the liaison unit.

Sarah pulled out her notebook, already brimming with ideas. "Let's start with weekly community meetings. We can rotate neighborhoods so we cover different areas consistently. It's about visibility and accessibility."

Ian agreed, adding, "And let's not forget about youth engagement. Summer's coming up; we could coordinate with local schools to set up workshops or safety seminars."

Their conversation was interrupted by a young officer, eager to be part of the new initiative. "Detectives, I heard about the liaison unit. I'd really like to be involved, especially with the youth workshops. I have some ideas that might resonate with the local teens."

"That's exactly the kind of initiative we're looking for," Sarah responded warmly. "Let's set up a time to discuss your ideas more fully."

The rest of the day was a blur of planning and discussions, with various officers bringing their insights and enthusiasm to the fledgling unit. The positive momentum was palpable, a stark contrast to the darker days of the Wolfe investigation.

As the sun began to set, casting a golden glow over the city, Ian and Sarah finally took a moment to breathe, standing by the window in their new office. "Look at that sunset, Sarah. It's a perfect end to a day like today."

Sarah watched the horizon, where the sky met the city's outline. "It's beautiful. Days like this, they remind me why we do this job. It's about more than just enforcing laws. It's about making a place where people can feel safe and valued."

The chapter closed with Ian and Sarah looking out over the city they had sworn to protect, ready to face the challenges of their new roles with the same dedication and resilience that had seen them through their toughest days. Their partnership, strengthened by adversity, was set to embark on this new journey, shaping a future where the community and the police could thrive together.

Conclusion

As the city of Willow's End basked in the glow of a new day, Detectives Ian Mercer and Sarah Langley stood together on the precinct's rooftop, overlooking the streets where they had battled darkness to bring light. They had witnessed the dawn of a renewed community, one that had been tested by manipulation and fear but had emerged stronger, bound by a newfound trust and cooperation between the police and the people they served.

The recent weeks had been a whirlwind of revelations and challenges, culminating in a sweeping crackdown on the manipulative network orchestrated by Dr. Adrian Wolfe. His arrest had sent shockwaves through the community, exposing the deep roots of his influence and the breadth of his deception. But it had also galvanized the city into action, sparking reforms and healing divisions that had long festered unseen.

"Ian, do you ever think about what would've happened if we hadn't caught Wolfe when we did?" Sarah asked, her voice a mix of reflection and relief.

Ian turned to her, his eyes thoughtful. "Every day. But then I remind myself that we did, and it's because we worked together, not just as partners, but with the whole community."

Sarah nodded, her gaze sweeping across the skyline. "It feels like we've turned a corner, doesn't it? Not just catching a criminal, but actually making a real change."

"That's the goal," Ian affirmed. "To not only stop the bad guys but to build something good in the place they left behind. It's about more than just solving cases. It's about building a legacy of trust and safety."

As they stood together, the sun climbed higher, shedding light on the city's streets, parks, and homes. Children played in the distance, their laughter a testament to the resilience of a community that had reclaimed its spirit from the shadows.

Below them, the precinct buzzed with activity. Officers and detectives moved with a sense of purpose, motivated by the successes of recent weeks and the positive changes already taking effect. New community outreach programs were in full swing, bridges were being built, and the police force was evolving, becoming more integrated with the people it served.

Ian glanced at Sarah, a smile breaking across his face. "You know, for the first time in a long time, I'm optimistic about the future."

"Me too," Sarah replied, returning his smile. "It feels like we're part of something bigger. Like we're not just reacting to the bad, but actively creating the good."

The chapter—and their monumental case—closed not with the echo of past struggles, but with the promise of a brighter future. Ian and Sarah, along with the whole of Willow's End, stood ready to face whatever challenges lay ahead, knowing that their unity was their strongest asset. As the city moved forward, it did so with a collective resolve, a shared commitment to vigilance and virtue, ensuring that the darkness would never again overshadow the light.